*He unfastened
and dipped the cool cloth
beneath the folds of her
elegant blouse.*

"That's nice," Leeza breathed. "I never would
have suspected you had it in you."

Daggert continued slowly, carefully, bringing her
heat down after the day's brutal ride through the
hot New Mexico desert. Her color was coming
back, giving her a peachy glow. He drifted his
fingers over the swell of her breasts and up the
arch of her shoulders and back down again.

She sighed.

He allowed his fingers to dip lower, cooling her.

Heating him.

Her eyes opened abruptly, and a gaze as blue
and deep as the coldest mountain lake met
his squarely. "Enjoying yourself?" she asked.

He gave a final slow swipe before pulling his
hand back. "I'm not dead," he said.

"Something to look forward to, then," she purred.

Dear Reader,

This is a month full of greats: great authors, great miniseries…great books. Start off with award-winning Marie Ferrarella's *Racing Against Time,* the first in a new miniseries called CAVANAUGH JUSTICE. This family fights for what's right—and their reward is lasting love.

The miniseries excitement continues with the second of Carla Cassidy's CHEROKEE CORNERS trilogy. *Dead Certain* brings the hero and heroine together to solve a terrible crime, but it keeps them together with love. Candace Irvin's latest features *A Dangerous Engagement*, and it's also the first SISTERS IN ARMS title, introducing a group of military women bonded through friendship and destined to find men worthy of their hearts.

Of course, you won't want to miss our stand-alone books, either. Marilyn Tracy's *A Warrior's Vow* is built around a suspenseful search for a missing child, and it's there, in the rugged Southwest, that her hero and heroine find each other. Cindy Dees has an irresistible Special Forces officer for a hero in *Line of Fire*—and he takes aim right at the heroine's heart. Finally, welcome new author Loreth Anne White, who came to us via our eHarlequin.com Web site. *Melting the Ice* is her first book—and we're all eagerly awaiting her next.

Enjoy—and come back next month for more exciting romantic reading, only from Silhouette Intimate Moments.

Leslie J. Wainger
Executive Editor

Please address questions and book requests to:
Silhouette Reader Service
U.S.: 3010 Walden Ave., P.O. Box 1325, Buffalo, NY 14269
Canadian: P.O. Box 609, Fort Erie, Ont. L2A 5X3

A Warrior's Vow
MARILYN TRACY

Silhouette®

INTIMATE MOMENTS™
Published by Silhouette Books
America's Publisher of Contemporary Romance

SILHOUETTE BOOKS

ISBN 0-373-27321-5

A WARRIOR'S VOW

MARILYN TRACY

Marilyn's books, which range in subject matter from classic women-in-jeopardy scenarios to fallen angels fighting to save the universe, have placed on several best-seller lists and earned her such awards as *Romantic Times* Career and Lifetime Achievement Awards, and Best of Series. She claims to speak Russian with fair fluency, Hebrew with appalling mistakes and enough Spanish to get her arrested at any border crossing. She lives with her sister in Roswell, New Mexico, where the only aliens they've seen thus far are the critters in their new home, a converted railroad warehouse.

For Dick Satterlee, a gentle warrior,
who is surely playing the guitar in a far better place.
And hopefully far better guitar.
With love…

Chapter 1

"You *could* talk to me," Leeza called out. "I'll bet that's allowed in the great tracker rule book. Something easy, like, 'How are you faring back there?' Not much of a commitment. You can just shout out your response anytime now."

The man riding in front of her didn't turn around or acknowledge her in any way. His horse, Stone—undoubtedly named after the man's heart—swished his tail as if he, at least, was aware a bedraggled woman followed behind and had been doing so for countless hours.

Leeza Nelson wished she could summon up a straight back and a glare on the off chance the man riding in front of her would turn around and actually say something to her. But he wasn't likely to wonder how she was holding up, and she wasn't remotely able to sit up straight anymore. Every inch of her body ached and she'd lost all sensation in her bottom some five hours and thirty confusing mesquite bushes back.

The tracker she followed like a cowed pup didn't seem to care that she felt worried sick about a nine-year-old jokester named Enrique, missing now for almost a full day. Tracker James Daggert had made it obvious her presence would only slow him down and that her lack of experience at riding western style was nothing but a nuisance.

From the moment she'd announced her intention of accompanying him to search for the missing boy, this high-dollar tracker, Daggert, had made it abundantly clear that Leeza Nelson's wants and needs were one step lower than the desires of a desert mouse carrying the Hanta virus.

She was aware that as far as Daggert was concerned, she'd foisted herself into the mission, and she could put up or shut up.

This tracker extraordinaire was after only one thing, apparently: finding little Enrique. When they'd set out on this incredible trek, Daggert's single-minded focus on the mission had made her feel grateful that she'd contracted the right man for the job. As the head of her own financial corporation, she knew the value of finding the best person to do each specific task.

Daggert's resistance to her accompanying him had vaguely pleased her, for she had considered his reluctance might indicate a dedication to his task. That she'd been unwilling to go along with his edicts revealed her own determination to find the child.

But now, five hours later, she'd decided the man wasn't dedicated, he was an unadulterated sadist.

"I hate this," she muttered to her horse's twitching ears. "I hate New Mexico. I hate horses. And right now, I hate little Enrique for running away. For that matter, I hate sunshine, dry grass, open fricking terrain, and most of all, I hate, positively *hate* James Daggert."

Her horse, a beast with the unlikely name of Lulubelle, whickered.

Stone, James Daggert's horse, gave a whinny in response.

Daggert reined in his horse and let loose an ear-splitting whistle.

Lulubelle took another couple of steps and stopped abruptly, still some fifteen feet behind Stone.

Leeza rocked in the saddle, one half a gasp away from sliding to the ground in a puddle of defeat. Pride alone kept her on the horse. The evil tracker she'd hired to search for Enrique would probably leave her lying facedown in the dust if she did fall off.

"I'll show him," she growled to the equally evil beast she straddled. "If he thinks Leeza Nelson will ever admit defeat, he's got another think coming."

The horse didn't answer aside from stomping one huge hoof.

On the northern horizon, a brown blur raced toward the man. The ball of brown soon proved to be James Daggert's dog, a dark setter with liquid brown eyes, named Sancho. Leeza was sure James Daggert had never had a nodding acquaintance with Cervantes's Don Quixote, for though he would probably fit some gothic notion of a romantic figure, he was not one to tilt at windmills in his lady's name. A dreamer he was *not*.

The sable-coated dog came to a shuddering stop and gazed up at his master with slavish adoration. His tongue lolled from his grinning mouth and his eyes never wavered from the man sitting ramrod straight in his saddle.

The tracker tossed something down that the gorgeous animal caught in midair, his tail beating a breeze above the dry New Mexico grasses. He gave a sharp bark.

Incredibly, the man murmured something to the dog. Sancho wagged his tail even harder. It was the first time Leeza had heard Daggert's voice since starting out on their search for Enrique shortly after nine o'clock that morning. The deep, mellifluous, curiously gentle tone didn't match the hard visage of the man. And yet it did—at least with the setter and the monstrously large horse, Stone.

"Oh, I get it," she snapped. "You'll talk to your horse and your dog but not to me. And if you say the dog has more sense, I'll brain you."

James Daggert didn't say anything.

Big surprise.

Mentally, Leeza shot an arrow of pure fury directly between his shoulder blades. He didn't shift his muscled back one iota.

He gave a flick of his hand and his dog shot off toward the far horizon.

Leeza urged Lulubelle ahead to flank Stone, determined to make the man speak to her. She'd tried almost everything else, so this time she turned a glittering smile in his direction, forcing herself to be pleasant, to charm the man into talking to her. "Does your dog have Enrique's scent?"

Daggert's eyes turned in her direction and he gave her an unreadable look before shifting his gaze back to the desert ahead of them. He could have been a rock carving of an Indian warrior, and she suspected his heritage was indeed Native American. It showed in his deeply tanned face, his long black hair. But the granite-hard expression chiseled on those sharp features came from the unapproachable man himself. Under that long-sleeved cotton shirt his shoulders seemed like chunks of boulders, his back as straight as a cliff face.

His jet-black hair wasn't covered by a cowboy hat, and he'd tied it back in a ponytail held by a strip of leather. Despite the heat of the noon sun, James Daggert seemed oblivious to its effects, as if he were truly carved of stone.

Then, as though he'd known she was still gaping at him, he turned his head to look at her directly. The only thing that spoke of any Caucasian heritage could be found in his eyes. Tawny, almost amber colored, they glittered like gemstones and were as enigmatic and alluring.

He didn't appear angry or irritated. But the shock of meeting his unusual eyes and finding that indecipherable expression turned on her made Leeza's knees literally quake. A shaft of purely visceral heat shot through her. For a woman used to reading all types of people quickly, with assurance and uncanny accuracy, she found herself wholly out of her depth.

He sees through me, she thought with a shiver of true fear.

She forced her back to straighten a little and summoned a small smile. *Be friendly to the man. You need him.* "Have you had the dog long?"

He said nothing. His gaze shifted from her eyes to her mouth, lingered there for a moment, then moved slowly back up again. For some reason, the look made that shaft of heat spread.

If she hadn't heard him speaking English very clearly at the ranch earlier, she might have assumed the man didn't speak her language. And she then thought, with some shock, that perhaps she didn't speak his—the language of tracking, of searching for a missing person.

Years ago, Leeza had sworn she wouldn't squirm around any man, and she wasn't about to make an exception for this tracker. "A Gorden setter, right?"

Leeza registered the fact that Daggert deliberately turned his gaze away from her and urged Stone to a brisk walk.

Gritting her teeth, she did the same.

"He's a remarkable dog," she stated stubbornly.

James Daggert paid her less attention than he would have a flea on that Hanta-virus-bearing mouse.

"The children back at Rancho Milagro have yellow Labrador mixes," she said. "Enrique loves them."

Daggert didn't so much as glance in her direction.

"You know, you don't have to talk to me. I

couldn't care less, in fact," she lied. "But I *know* little Enrique. I could probably tell you a thing or two that might help us find him. Like where he might be going? However, you're the great tracker genius, so I'll concede the issue.

"I'm not even complaining about having to sit on this wildly uncomfortable western-style saddle you made the hands at the ranch put on this horse, despite the fact that I'm used to riding English. But I'll tell you what I really don't get—"

He leaned forward suddenly and his horse broke into a hard gallop. Within seconds, he was at least a football field's length ahead of her.

She sighed. "What I don't get is why you make my knees turn to water just looking at you."

Her horse nickered, as if laughing at her.

Seeing the shadows lengthen across the desert and knowing the night would soon plummet them into darkness, Daggert pulled back on Stone's reins and waited for the woman to catch up to him.

She did, but she didn't stop as her horse came abreast his. Her shoulders were slumped and her head drooped. Her eyes were open but glassy with exhaustion. Her lips moved, but he couldn't make out what she was saying. The eager horse and spent woman moved on past him.

He urged Stone forward and grabbed hold of her slackened reins. If her horse had seen a snake or had stumbled even once, she'd have tumbled off. As it was, with his stopping the horse, she nearly slid down, anyway.

He swore beneath his breath and swiftly dismounted. He dropped Stone's reins to the ground, knowing the big horse wouldn't move so much as a step away. Keeping hold of her horse's reins, he circled the mare and reached up for Leeza Nelson.

She was still muttering, and, closer to her now, he could hear her strangely lifeless recitation of facts about her missing charge, the boy he'd been hired to find. "He likes to draw. He likes to swim. He likes pancakes. He likes puppies. He likes practical jokes. He likes to draw. He likes to swim. He likes…"

She was leaning forward over the saddle horn, still rocking slightly, muttering in a strange rhythm, seemingly unaware that they'd stopped. Her beautiful face was pasty and her knuckles even whiter.

Without a word, Daggert wrapped her horse's reins around his wrist and dislodged her nerveless feet from the stirrups she'd had the men at the ranch raise a couple of inches so that she could pretend she was riding English style. She issued a small sound either of protest or of pain as her feet dangled free and blood rushed to them.

"Come on down now," he said, holding up his hands to her.

"He likes to draw," she murmured.

Daggert felt a cold knife slip into the hard casing surrounding his heart. *"Daddy, see what I drew! It's you, see?"* A stick figure with long hair and a horse the size of a mountain had been the last picture Donny ever drew.

"Come," he said to the woman.

She turned her gaze in his direction and he saw

understanding slowly filter through her fatigue. "We're stopping," she said. It was a statement of profound need rather than a question.

"Come down," he said, and when she didn't move, he added, "I've got you."

He saw her try to swing her leg over the back of the horse, but between that damned foolish way of hitching up her stirrups—trying to ride English style across a desert for hours—and the long day they'd put in, she couldn't manage to make her muscles work for her.

He gripped her elbow and gave a sharp tug. She slid from the horse, straight into his waiting arms. As her mount sidled away, Daggert staggered back a step, the reins cutting at his wrist and pulling him sideways. But he didn't release her. He held her to his chest, too aware of her trembling body cradled against his.

He could smell some elusive fragrance wafting from her hair, and above it, the familiar scent of sunshine and bone-dry September desert in southeastern New Mexico. She'd closed her eyes, and he was glad of that because he'd already discovered they were such an incredible blue that they hurt a man to look too deeply into them.

As feisty as she'd been all day, he half anticipated her demanding he get his dirty hands off her. Instead, she turned her head to his chest. "Oh, thank God," she murmured. "Thank you. Thank you."

Instinctively, his arms tightened around her.

He carried her a few paces, dragging the reluctant horse behind them, then gently sank to one knee to set her down on the lee side of a sandy mound. She murmured in protest as he pulled his arms away, but she didn't open her eyes.

Daggert waited for a few seconds, making sure she wasn't going to slump face first into the sand. She merely leaned her blond head back against the earth and sighed.

He unwound her horse's reins from his wrist, and, ignoring the abrasion left by the leather ties, led the animal back toward Stone. After a quick survey of the area, Daggert loosely tied both horses to a scraggly branch of a scrub oak. He pulled one of the saddlebags free from Stone's many packs and quickly withdrew both a canteen of water and some moistened towelettes.

The woman hadn't moved from her sandy bed and only shook her head when he knelt beside her again.

"Go away, sadist," she murmured.

"Here's some water."

"I'll bet it's poisoned," she said. "You'd make better time if you left me for dead."

"Drink," he said. He lifted her cramped hands and frowned at the chafed skin on her palms and between her fingers. She'd obviously gripped both the saddle horn and the reins with that same fierce intensity she put into those knifelike glares he'd felt against his back most of the day.

He held the canteen to her lips and cupped the base of her neck in his hand. Her soft, fluffy cap of hair played with the fine hairs on the back of his hand. She resisted at first, then, as the cold liquid trickled across her lips and down her chin, she roused sufficiently to swallow. When she might have gulped it and caused her stomach to cramp, he pulled the canteen away.

"I'm going to wake up and this will all have been a nightmare. Enrique will be home, eating dinner. I won't be out in the desert with some stranger who hates women," she said clearly, if not very logically.

Daggert carefully sealed the water container and set it aside before opening one of the towelettes. With as much gentleness as he might have used on one of his animals, he wiped her brow, her cheeks and the hollow of her slender, sharply marked collarbone.

She moved a little, arching her back to accommodate him. He continued slowly, carefully, bringing her heat down and erasing the dust of a day's ride from her lovely skin. Her color, he saw, was coming back, giving her a peachy glow in the dusky light. As he continued to bathe her with the cool cloth, he saw her fingers finally begin to relax.

"That's nice," she breathed. "I never would have suspected you had it in you."

He unbuttoned the top button of her elegant blouse and dipped the cool cloth beneath the folds, drawing it near the swell of her breasts, up the arch of each shoulder and back down again.

She sighed once more.

He allowed his fingers to dip a bit lower, cooling her. Heating him.

Her eyelids opened abruptly and eyes as blue and deep as the coldest mountain lake met his squarely. "Enjoying yourself?" she asked.

He gave a final slow swipe before pulling his hand back. "I'm not dead," he said.

"Something to look forward to, then," she purred.

He pushed himself erect and walked away from her. He didn't look back. If he did, he knew he would stare. Even exhausted as she was, her reserves depleted, Daggert knew that short of the silver screen, he'd never seen a woman as staggeringly beautiful and as perfectly formed as Leeza Nelson. As tall as a fashion model and as willowy as any young tree in springtime, she nevertheless filled out her snazzy clothes in all the right places.

And those eyes were as blue as liquid cobalt and as icy as a pond in late winter. One plunge and a man would either drown or feel reborn. Or be killed for getting too close to the edge.

And where everything else about her seemed sleek and elegant, her hair was a slightly mussed cap of blond wisps that seemed to call for his touch. When it had teased the back of his hand as he helped her drink the water, he'd had to force himself not to let his fingers tangle in that spun silk.

The only thing that didn't match that picture of total perfection had been the brief, glittering blaze of fury he'd glimpsed in her when he'd countermanded her saddle choice early in the day.

Leeza Nelson, female magnate of some big-shot corporation back east, and one of the co-owners of the huge Rancho Milagro, a miracle foster children's home in the middle of the desert, obviously wasn't used to having anyone question her commands. He'd only had to be around her for fifteen minutes back at the ranch to know she issued them like royal edicts, a half smile of authority on her princess lips, when no smile existed in her eyes.

He'd found just a little too much pleasure in watching her fight to keep her finely boned face from revealing her anger. And he had far too much interest in speculating what her do-as-I-tell-you mouth might feel like beneath his.

Daggert had to give her credit. She'd ridden for eight hours straight without a single complaint—except about his silence. She'd left her comfortable ranch, following a complete stranger, a man who many called crazy and worse, to look for a runaway boy who'd been only recently deposited at the ranch.

Leeza could have stayed put and called in a host of law enforcement types—Lord knew that with one of her ranch partners married to a federal marshal, she could have had her pick of half a dozen agencies. She could have simply waited with the others at *Rancho Milagro,* trusting fate to deliver the little boy back home safely. She could have directed the ranch hands to scour the land, searching for the boy who had undoubtedly already run away from a dozen different foster homes.

But Leeza Nelson hadn't done any of those things. She'd sent the ranch hands searching in the predawn hours. She'd directed law enforcement to check bus stations and highways. And she'd decided she needed to find the boy herself, with the aid of one half-breed Apache, a notorious tracker named Daggert. That she'd taken the trouble to find the best told him a lot about her.

And the set look on her lovely face as she'd refused to back down when he'd announced he worked alone had told him something, as well.

"Not this time," she'd said coolly. And any man in his right mind would have shivered and asked for a parka right about then.

She hadn't pleaded, or cajoled him into agreeing; she'd just ordered a horse saddled and a pack prepared. She'd given orders like a general on a campaign and had only shot him that one furious glare at his countermanding her saddle choice.

He'd made it clear he wasn't going to slow down for her, that if she was determined to force herself on him, he wasn't going to nursemaid her. If he was going to find this little boy, he couldn't afford to stop and smell flowers along the way.

And damned if she hadn't matched him step for grueling step all day.

And despite her overt weariness, she'd still summoned enough spunk to slap him down when he'd slipped his hand beneath her blouse.

With his back to her, he smiled. The lady had grit, he'd give her that, even if she didn't have the faintest notion of what was what. His smile faded. She was under the impression that she'd hired him to find her missing runaway. That was true, in a way, but there was far more to it than that.

He'd have done it for free, as half the people of Carlsbad would have told her if she'd asked. He was the person everyone called when someone was missing. Not because he was lucky, but because he was relentless. And because he had another agenda.

He loosened her saddle and slid it from the mare's back. He did the same for Stone, setting all the packs to the south side of the sandy arroyo he'd chosen for the night's camp, a place safe for that evening, as no storms threatened. It was September and even in drought years rain always fell in that month, the transition from summer into autumn. They'd had rain the night before the boy ran away and they would again in the next four days. Knowing that wasn't magic on Daggert's part; it was courtesy of the National Weather Service.

"Hello?"

He turned in her direction.

She was on her cell phone. She'd spent the better part of the first stage of their journey with the little black instrument pressed against her ear, jabbering into it as if it and not people might conjure up the missing boy.

Daggert went back to setting up the camp as she leaned forward, apparently seeking better reception. She'd better have a great conversation tonight, for the Guadalupe Mountains were renowned for interrupting cell phone service. Unless on cliff sides or in high mountain meadows, wireless communication was almost nil in the Guadalupes, and there wasn't any other kind shy of smoke signals.

"No, not a sign of him," he heard her say.

Daggert didn't even bother to shake his head. There had been plenty of signs of Enrique's progress; he just hadn't pointed them out to the lady from back east. A piece of a tortilla covered with ants. A chewing gum wrapper. Hoofprints from the boy's horse—

noted because Rancho Milagro used the same farrier that most of the county did, and this particular black-smith liked to bend one horseshoe nail backward, leaving his distinct signature every time a horse stepped on anything but pure asphalt.

Daggert and the woman were still quite a way behind their prey, but narrowing the gap considerably. The boy hadn't been able to push his horse very swiftly in the dark the night before. With luck they might catch up with him by noon the following day.

"Okay, you know my number. Call me if you hear anything," she said, and hung up without a farewell. A no-frills woman. A woman used to running things her way. And probably getting them her way, as well.

Daggert thought that, given a couple of millennia, they might actually find they had a few things in common.

"Are we really stopping for the night?" she asked him with more than a hint of accusation in her tone. "Shouldn't we just take a rest and keep looking?"

He shook his head and continued setting up camp. Again he felt a reluctant stab of admiration. Grit? The woman had more than mere grit. She had class. She couldn't have ridden another step, but here she was, ready to get back out there.

Better than she did, Daggert understood the need to continue the search, no matter the hour, no matter the lack of light. The ice princess only believed Enrique Dominguez had run away from Rancho Milagro.

Daggert knew she didn't have a clue what dangers lurked out there. Like Dorothy in *The Wizard of Oz,* she didn't know she had come in contact with lions, tigers and bears. She had no way of knowing that no one, especially little Enrique, was safe from the dangers lurking in the Guadalupes.

She didn't have the foggiest notion of what might have befallen the boy just a few yards outside the fence surrounding the massive headquarters of the children's home—not from rattlesnakes and other animals, though those were prevalent enough. Worse things than nature and nature's creatures lurked among grasses, stunted trees and thorny shrubs.

But Daggert wasn't about to tell her what really scared him. He didn't want to have a hysterical woman on his hands. Not that Leeza Nelson seemed the type for histrionics. But she was still laboring under the idea that the boy she followed was simply running away from a foster care situation, if not—if the ranch hands were to believed—from Leeza Nelson personally.

Daggert knew that accepting such an easy explanation for the boy's continued absence was almost like selecting his gravestone. Daggert should know, he'd lost his own son that way.

Having finished taking care of Stone, he tended Leeza's mare. He hummed a little as he worked and, between the brushing and the tuneless susurration, both horses relaxed their bunched muscles and gently whickered their thanks.

He decided he couldn't call the mare by her given name; Lulubelle was a ridiculous handle. Noble creatures demanded dignified names. He ran his hand down her withers and on down her legs, feeling the powerful muscles ripple beneath his palm. No sign of her being winded, no overt indication of lather, no swelling... Like Stone, she was in prime condition. ''I'll call you Belle,'' he told her. ''You're as beautiful as your rider.''

Belle nodded her head as if agreeing with him.

Chapter 2

In the fading light, Leeza watched Daggert touching Lulubelle, and knew a pang of something akin to envy. The man ran his hands over the horse as a lover might, firmly, with sure intent and deliberate strokes. He knew just where to touch the beast to gentle her, to soothe her, to make her understand his wishes. He applied light pressure to her knee joints and, one by one, she lifted her legs for him. He stroked her neck, whispering to her, and she swayed into his embrace. His hand traveled every part of her and she trembled beneath his touch.

By the time Daggert turned around, Leeza's mouth had gone dry once more, but this time exhaustion had nothing whatsoever to do with it. Her face, usually schooled to reveal nothing, must have showed her every thought because he checked his stride, and his golden eyes seemed to sharpen.

At that moment, she couldn't have spoken if her life depended on it. He looked every inch the warrior she'd imagined him when she'd stepped out on the veranda earlier that day and coolly announced she was accompanying him on the search for Enrique Dominguez.

But there was more than the warrior in his eyes now. His frozen stance reminded her of something feral, wild. A black wolf, perhaps—wary, dangerous and dominant. The sudden heat in his gaze only underscored the impression. Then he moved again, his stride fluid and muscled, deliberately turning his gaze away from her.

She wondered if she'd imagined what had just happened, then questioned if he'd provided the show with the horse just to drive her crazy. She shook her head. He couldn't have. He would have to have eyes in the back of his head to know she'd sat there slack-jawed, imagining the touch of his hand on her body instead of the horse's.

She'd simply been affected by the day's intense heat.

The difficult ride.

The worry over Enrique.

And the fact that she was wholly out of her element.

Her reaction was nothing more than these things. Absolutely nothing.

But none of those reasons explained away the fire his gaze had lit inside her.

To her relief, Daggert's dog, Sancho, came running up then, his long, black-spotted tongue lolling. He spat out a branch of some kind at his master's feet and barked twice before sitting down and panting heavily.

Leeza blushed when Daggert pulled a plastic bowl and cup from one of his packs and poured a little canteen water into each. She'd drunk directly from the canteen. He set the bowl down for the dog and quickly quenched his own thirst. When Sancho barked, he shook his head and picked up the bowl.

"Fire first, dinner later," he told the dog gently.

He carefully replaced the items in his packs before beginning to gather large river rocks from the arroyo's sandy banks. The dog settled down in the sand beside the saddles, lay his head on Daggert's tooled leather seat and gave a great sigh. Like his master, the dog didn't glance her way.

Leeza looked up to find Daggert standing less than six inches away from her. She hadn't heard him move. He held out his hand.

She looked at his callused palm as if it might hold snakes. He waited. She placed her stiff fingers in his and was startled by the contact. He might as well have kissed her, so intimate was the sensation of their fingers touching. She could feel the heat of his skin, the roughness of his calluses and some indefinable psychic energy emanating from him.

And when his fingers wrapped around hers and he effortlessly pulled her to her feet, inches from his rock-hard body, she felt the impact arrow through her. She tried removing her hand, but he didn't release her. She gave him a startled glance and found he was staring at her with a fixed, almost hard look. A wolf's look.

A flutter of fear and unbridled need made her breath catch.

And still he held her hand, not squeezing it, but not letting her go, either.

"That's hilarious," she drawled, but she felt something inside her quaking, both with that strange fear and something else she'd never experienced before.

He said nothing, though he continued to look at her as if forcing her to read his thoughts, understand the meaning of his touch. Abruptly, he let her go.

Her hand hung in the air for a moment, as if he'd hypnotized her and no power on earth would let her lower her limb. Then she jerked it down to her side. It seemed to tingle, but she resisted the urge to look at it. Or at him.

Daggert stacked the river rocks in a circle for the night's campfire. Even as he performed the methodical task, he felt the woman's presence. When he'd turned from her horse to see her watching him, with a fire flickering in her gaze and her lips parted and her fingertips resting against her pulsing throat, he'd felt a fuse light inside him. Who'd have thought such a cool customer would have such a look in her eyes?

Could it be she didn't even know it? Her mouth had snapped shut and her eyes had widened as if she saw something in his face. Maybe she'd spent so many years playing the ice princess that she'd convinced herself she was just that.

He'd told her she wasn't dead, but until he'd held

her in his arms, even if just to keep her from falling down, he might as well have been six feet under. When little Donny died, something in him had been murdered, too. The crippling guilt and scarcely checked rage had turned him away from everyone, everything he knew.

He should have made sure Donny hadn't walked home alone from his friend's house. He should have found the boy in minutes. He should have tracked the fiend who'd taken his only son. He should have found the monster and eviscerated him.

Sometimes Daggert wondered if he'd have been okay if his ex-wife had blamed him, too. But she hadn't. She'd nearly drowned in her grief, but she hadn't blamed her tracker husband, hadn't ever said a word to imply she harbored anything but sympathy for his torment. But even with her acceptance, Alma hadn't been able to get past the terrible pain rioting just below the surface of James Daggert. He'd understood when she gave up one day and left him in the canyons of his own despair. She deserved a life, deserved to find some measure of happiness. He sure as hell couldn't give it to her anymore.

He thought of the woman who had ridden behind him all day, and of her determination to find Enrique. The fleeting thought that she might not give up on him flashed through Daggert's mind. He shook his head. That was crazy thinking.

Still, he found some grim satisfaction in knowing he wasn't dead to sensation, that his body, if no other part of him, could still be swamped with restless need, however painful. He smiled wryly, suspecting he'd be hurting plenty by the conclusion of this particular mission.

He thought about her sad little litany of surface facts about Enrique Dominguez, the way she'd repeated them like a talisman against her exhaustion. He'd done the same with Donny. Not reciting all the little things he knew about the boy—those were carved in his heart—but details about his death.

The fact that no one had seen anyone unusual that day was significant all by itself. A little boy on his way home from a friend's house didn't wind up some forty miles away, mangled beyond recognition. Daggert knew that people had seen someone, all right— someone they *knew*. But because they knew him, they'd forgotten they'd seen him. Because he belonged there. Like fences, like flowerbeds, like grass.

Someone Donny knew. Someone Daggert knew.

Everyone became suspect. Everyone became potential child killers. And his litany became, "Who is it? Who do I know who's capable of murder? Who did everyone see that day and not even notice? *The butcher, the baker, the candlestick maker?*"

He understood the need to focus. He understood litanies. They drove fear away and kept despair at bay.

After he laid the fire and lit it, he pulled out his collapsible water buckets, filled them and set them down in front of the horses. He doled two scoops each of molasses oats into canvas feed bags, and after the horses had drunk their fill, slipped a makeshift chuck-wagon on to each horse's head.

He hoped he and the woman would find the boy

the next day, not just for the child's sake. He hadn't planned on feeding two horses, and had brought enough oats for one, for only five days. At this rate, they would last only three full days without supplemental supplies, and it took nearly that long to reach the upper mountains.

The only sounds that could be heard were the distant cry of a nighthawk, horses munching oats and the fire crackling in the chilly desert night. Into that companionable quiet, he heard Leeza ask, ''What do you want me to do?''

''Sit,'' he said, pulling two dinner packets from one of his saddlebags. ''Watch out for goat heads.''

''*What?*''

''Stickers. Shaped like goat heads.''

''Oh. Thanks.''

Daggert set a pot of water on the broad, flat rocks he'd placed in the middle of their fire circle. At some three thousand feet on the high desert plain, water wouldn't take long to boil.

He added the already cooked meals in their little plastic bags to the churning water. When they were heated through, he plucked them from the pot with his pocketknife and, slicing them open, dumped the contents on to the aluminum plates he'd set out earlier.

As he worked, Leeza didn't say a single word, not even muttering snide comments when she thought he couldn't hear her, as she had much of the day. He turned to look at her and found her staring at the flames, silent tears coursing down her beautiful face.

He briefly closed his eyes. Even if he were the most

talkative man in the world, he wouldn't have known what to say now. He said nothing, pretending he hadn't seen her anguish, and dug in one of the packs again, withdrawing a container of salt and pepper and a couple of napkins.

The race for space travel had vastly improved simple pleasures on earth. Even the sorriest excuse for a cook could rustle up a decent meal with freeze-dried ingredients or precooked entrées, a pot of hot water and a few spices carefully packed in a plastic bag. Within minutes, he set a plate of beef stew out for Sancho and two more of pasta primavera for Leeza and himself.

With a wary glance at her, he held out her plate. Most signs of tears were gone, but she didn't respond.

"You'll feel better if you eat something," he said.

She reached for the plate then, and he let out a pent-up breath as he handed her a fork. She stirred the pasta around but didn't make any move to eat. "Enrique's only nine," she said.

He waited. Donny had been seven. He would be seven forever. *"He's growing up, Alma. Let him walk home alone."*

"And he's afraid of thunder."

Daggert forked in a mouthful of pasta and chewed silently. *"Daddy? You won't let the lightning hurt me, right?"*

"He plays practical jokes." She gave a watery chuckle. "He put a paper sack filled with dry leaves in the back of a dresser drawer so I'd think there was a rattlesnake in it when I opened the drawer. It worked."

She was silent as Daggert took several bites, then said, "Everyone thinks Enrique dislikes me."

Daggert stirred the fire, and the coals in his memory. *"You're too hard on him, James. He's just a little boy."*

"Do you want to know why?"

He set his knife aside.

"They—everyone from my best friends to the housekeeper—thought I was too hard on the children. All the children. But mostly Enrique."

"Why?"

"Do you mean why does everyone think I'm too hard, why was I too hard or why Enrique in particular?" she asked.

"You choose," Daggert answered, amazed at her ability to split meanings.

"You sound like a psychiatrist."

He didn't say anything, thinking she couldn't know how ironic that sounded, due to the fact that a host of psychiatrists hadn't been able to put him together again. *All the king's horses and all the king's men...* One of Donny's favorite nursery rhymes.

"Okay, I don't believe anything can be accomplished without hard work. And it's my experience that children need strict rules and guidelines. It's how I was raised, and I'm fully aware of the benefits of such a firm hand at the helm. And why Enrique in particular? Because he's smart, because he's lazy. Because he's vulnerable, and vulnerability only makes victims."

"Being vulnerable is a liability, then?"

"I'm tired," she said suddenly, and handed him

the plate of uneaten food. "I think I'll pass on the rest of this session."

He handed her plate back. "It was a hard ride and a long day. You'd better eat something."

"Really, I couldn't."

"But you will."

She gave him a cold look that let him understand he'd have to wrestle her down and force-feed her before she'd concede.

He sighed. "Lady, I won't have time tomorrow to take you back to the ranch when you faint from hunger. You don't have enough meat on your bones to go a day without food. It's a matter of simple mathematics. The boy already has a twelve-hour head start on us. Add another eight or nine hours and the kid's been out in the open for almost twenty-four hours already. We have to catch up with him soon, and we won't be able to if I'm busy picking you up off the ground."

Though Leeza watched him warily, Daggert didn't look at her as he bent over his own plate and resumed his careful eating. She dipped up a forkful of the pasta and tasted it. She was surprised at how delicious it was. If Daggert dared smile, she'd give the plate of pasta to his dog rather than continue to eat it herself, but he didn't. He merely finished his dinner in a silence that almost felt easy.

And she was hungrier than she'd thought, for within seconds, her plate was empty, too.

"Thank you," she said finally, relinquishing it into his hands. "You were right, I was hungry."

He nodded and moved away from the fire, but not

before Leeza had caught a sober look of something that might have been sympathy in his gaze. Sympathy or an almost reluctant compassion. For some odd reason, the notion of his possessing any compassion unnerved her. It was far easier to think of him as rude and bullying and harder than nails than to see him as a human being with human emotions.

After she'd warily used the meager facilities he'd set up behind a low scrub oak, and availed herself of some of the remaining hot water, she turned her back on him and carefully, stiffly, removed her coat, blouse and boots.

Never one for voyeurism, Daggert tried turning his gaze to the fire, but failed miserably when he heard the rasp of her jeans zipper. Her legs went on forever.

"Goddamn," he said.

She stiffened but didn't turn around. "What?"

"I burned myself," he lied. Or was he telling the abject truth?

Amazing him, she pulled on a pair of red satin pajamas. She might as well have been at some fancy motel instead of camping out in the desert on a mission to find a runaway kid. What had possessed her housekeeper to pack such a ridiculous item?

"Good night," she said, slipping into her sleeping bag.

"Right," he said, feeling as if he'd fallen down Alice's rabbit hole.

"Sleep well," she murmured.

Thinking about her in that getup, he'd be lucky if he ever slept again.

Chapter 3

*F*rom atop the highest peak in the rising foothills, the hunter, as he thought of himself, was able to see for miles in all directions. With powerful binoculars at his eyes, he could easily discern Leeza Nelson in red pajamas that made her look as if she'd dressed herself in flame. He saw Daggert moving around the fire, banking it, careful as ever.

The tracker hadn't been so careful four years ago, had he?

Turning his binoculars to the north, he spied the would-be fire of his newest prey. Everything in him itched to move forward, to catch the boy and teach him a lesson about crossing boundaries. He'd taught many before.

But he shifted his gaze back to the woman slipping into her sleeping bag. The hunter wondered if Leeza

Nelson knew that people called Daggert the Cassandra of the desert, always crying murder and never finding enough evidence to prove it. He wondered if she'd heard that Daggert was the man everyone trusted and no one believed.

The woman should have given up by now, but she'd stayed with Daggert throughout the day, even if she posted in her saddle, English style.

She didn't know about boundaries, either. Maybe it was time she was taught a lesson.

The man wondered if he should flip a coin. The woman or the boy? Heads the woman, tails the child. If he played his cards right—and he was one hell of a card player—he might have the opportunity to teach both of them.

He didn't need a fire. His thoughts of what he would do to them warmed him thoroughly.

Leeza was wholly spent, tired in places she'd never been aware of before, yet sleep eluded her.

The night stars seemed heavy, as if straining against invisible reins to streak to the earth. She could pick out the Big and Little Dippers, Cassiopeia and the Seven Sisters. In another month she'd be able to find Orion's belt, she knew a portend of the coming winter.

She'd shown Enrique the constellations one night about two weeks earlier. He'd studied them carefully, trying to see patterns in the myriad twinkling lights until he finally learned the few she could always find.

''My parents are up there,'' he'd said.

Assuming he'd meant ''in heaven,'' Leeza had had

to clench her hands in her lap to keep from wrapping
her arms around the little boy who'd lost both parents
at such an early age.

Just as she had.

But no one had coddled her. Not in any of the
foster homes she'd been shuffled in and out of in her
early years. Not in the tidy home John and Cora Nelson had brought her to when she was nine. Enrique's
age exactly.

"Emotionalism is a waste of time," her adoptive
father had said on more than one occasion, usually
when her eyes were brimming with tears over some
imagined hurt. "It reveals a lack of precise thinking."

Looking at the stars now, out in the middle of a
vast desert wilderness, inches from a hard stranger
who was kind to his animals if not to the woman
who'd hired him, Leeza found herself wishing that
she'd drawn Enrique onto her lap and held him close.
If she had given just that small measure of comfort,
would he have opted to stay at the ranch and not run
away into the darkness?

Her partners, Corrie and Jeannie, fellow orphans
and sisters in heart if not blood, had entered the Rancho Milagro venture with their arms wide open for
the children arriving at the foster-care facility. Leeza
had agreed to become a partner in the project for two
reasons: Jeannie had needed something to do after her
husband and baby had been killed in a senseless ac-
cident, and because Leeza herself truly believed in the
value of a firm guiding hand for children who were
lost, for whatever reason.

She just hadn't expected it to be so hard. She had

assumed they would hire a few teachers, set the children on the straight and narrow, and guide them to understand how they all had an opportunity to make something of their lives. Much as John and Cora Nelson had done with her.

Instead, Jeannie had expected them to actually live on the premises, to give up their lives in Washington, D.C. and move to the remote location north of Carlsbad, New Mexico. Jeannie had come first, overseeing the renovation of the ramshackle place. Corrie came next, to find a new life for herself and the children she loved.

Finally, reluctantly, Leeza had arrived. She'd given the ranch a halfhearted try, but in truth, she was eager to get back to her business deals and mergers. The venture at the ranch seemed chaotic to her, out of control, and not just because the state and federal regulations kept them hamstrung. It was the children who created the biggest problem for Leeza.

Children scarcely out of diapers, angry teenagers and kids like sad-eyed little Enrique had been deposited at Rancho Milagro, the last stop in a string of broken homes and hearts. Each one seemed to weigh on Leeza's soul, though she'd never admitted it before now. And little Enrique with his questing mind, that oddly shaped scar on his forehead—a permanent reminder that man's inhumanity to children persisted no matter how many laws were changed—his quirky sense of humor and those too-old eyes, had gotten under her skin more than the others.

Was that the reason she'd ridden him harder, pushed him with greater determination? So much so that she'd driven him away from the ranch of miracles?

Exhaustion and fear had brought unfamiliar tears earlier that night. Luckily, the rock-hard Daggert hadn't seen them, or if he had, he'd pretended otherwise. Now her worry over the little runaway had driven her grief deep inside again, to a lonely place of roiling emotions, with no relief or release.

She would find him. She had to. That's all there was to it.

She reviewed the situation with a cold dispassion. Mentally evaluating any given situation was an exercise she'd learned early in childhood, and had been drilled into her by her adoptive parents. Mental precision kept fear at bay.

Bracingly, she told herself that a day's absence was not so long on a very big ranch. And Enrique had a coat, a blanket and a horse named Dandelion.

And though he couldn't know it, he had her, a really smart dog and a master tracker named James Daggert going after him.

"Damn it, lady, go to sleep." Daggert's voice was strangely soft. "You're doing the best you can."

She closed her eyes against the weight of the stars, her fears for Enrique and the closeness of the man lying not two feet from her. Her last conscious thought was to wonder how Daggert had known she was awake. And how he'd known to say the one thing that would allow her to relax enough to sleep.

She woke what seemed seconds later to the sound of something creeping around the camp. Even as fear made her breath catch in her throat, hope that it might be Enrique flooded through her. But on the very real chance it was a bear, she opened her eyes the merest bit.

At first she couldn't see anything in the darkness, then she made out James Daggert's silhouette against a wall of dimming stars. She thought he might be praying, he stood so still, facing the thinnest slice of predawn light on the horizon. He drew a deep breath and expelled it slowly. His exhalation hung in the air, and for some reason, it was a lonely sight—man, stars and cloud of warm breath against a black sky.

The chill of the September morning nipped at her cheeks, and she huddled in her sleeping bag, realizing she'd actually slept all night. As the sky lightened, she watched Daggert move about the camp.

He packed his things neatly and with considerable skill. He studied the camp with the eyes of a drill sergeant inspecting a parade troop. She'd seen his attention to detail the day before, but watching him when he was unaware of her gave her the opportunity to see that nothing about his movements was wasted. He was, in his way, an efficiency expert.

She wondered if the precision was a matter of survival. It certainly was in her world. Lack of attention to every nuance of a venture was the ruination of a venture capitalist, and she was one of the very best.

Leeza suspected Daggert left nothing to chance because lack of forethought on his part might mean certain death for him or the person he sought.

His horse nickered at him and he whispered for Stone to be quiet.

Leeza, buried in her warm sleeping bag, smiled beneath the covers.

She'd never taken the time to watch a man prepare for his day. Any encounters she'd had in the past had ended with a yawn, a polite good-night and the firm shutting of her door as her companion departed. Waking up with a man seemed too great an intimacy, too close to an emotional entanglement.

Not that she was technically waking up with James Daggert. She stopped smiling.

The horse nickered again and Daggert moved toward him, running his broad palm over the large, rangy sorrel. He murmured something and the animal rumbled in appreciation.

"Soon, old man," Daggert said softly.

Leeza could hear true affection in his voice, as if he and the horse had been through many rough times together and the dangers they'd faced had forged an unbreakable bond between them. Watching them, she tried imagining feeling the powerful muscles rippling beneath her palm. Instead, her mind substituted Daggert's bare shoulders. She closed her eyes.

"Good morning, Belle, you beauty, you."

Her eyes flew open. And she blushed, realizing that velvet voice hadn't been addressing her, but rather her horse.

The renamed Belle pawed the ground, as if answering him.

Leeza sighed as Daggert hefted the thick saddle pad, then the hated saddle, onto Belle's back and cinched it securely. He packed her saddle as carefully as he had his own. When all was aboard the horse, with the exception of Leeza and her sleeping bag, he gave Belle a slice of apple.

The setter, apparently knowing Daggert's ritual, came up, wagging his tail and whining at his master. Daggert ran his hand down the dog's soft neck. Leeza thought she'd never seen a man so completely comfortable around animals. It was as if he shared a telepathic communication with them.

"No use hurrying, Sancho. We have a half hour before full daylight, and if I know women—and contrary to your experience of me, I've known a few in my time—the lady won't be ready, anyway."

Leeza could have sworn the dog grinned as his feathered tail swept the earth. James ran his hands down the full length of the dog's back, and Leeza wriggled even as the animal did.

Sancho barked.

Leeza groaned.

"She's awake," Daggert said. "Close your eyes now or her red pajamas will blind you."

Daggert firmly believed that a good ninety-nine percent of the human population looked a bit worse for wear after a night out in the open. Not Leeza Nelson.

She looked as if she'd just stepped from a penthouse apartment, freshly showered, powdered and having had a manicure following a massage. Instead, she'd come around a scraggly mesquite bush and used towelettes for a bath. The only telltale sign that she'd been horseback riding most of the day before was her slightly stiff walk as she approached the campfire.

He pointed to the coffeepot, then poured some for her before she reached for it without a pot holder. She gave him a dazzling smile that made him wish he'd packed a Kevlar vest.

Not trusting her friendliness—she hadn't struck him as a hail-fellow-well-met sort of person—he busied himself unrolling a chamois cloth and spreading out the items Sancho had collected the day before. He sat studying them.

"What's all this?" Leeza asked brightly.

"Clues," he said.

"Explain, please," she said. Not a question, but a command, even if she had softened it. That do-it-my-way attitude again.

"Sancho brought them in last night." He held up the branch of scrub oak the dog had carried in his jaws. He pointed to the thistles that had been embedded in his silky coat. "Russian thistle and tumbleweed. Broken, but still fresh, see? And these? Bits of chamisa. Another gum wrapper."

"His path," she said, a note of wonder in her voice. "That's the path Sancho took—following Enrique?"

Daggert couldn't help but look at her. Her logic wasn't what snared him; it was the honest note of awe in her voice. Luckily, she wasn't gazing back at him. She was beaming at his Sancho.

"You're a good dog," she said. "A very, very good dog."

Sancho rose and came to her, tail beating against Daggert's back.

Daggert was stunned. He'd never seen Sancho approach anyone other than himself. The mutt always seemed to maintain a purely business relationship on their mission, eschewing fraternization with the clients, just like his master.

Daggert found he preferred things that way. He pushed Sancho's tail aside, but instead of moving away, the dog merely gave Daggert a happy grin and sat down beside the woman.

She looped an arm around his back, scratched at his ears and asked the dog, "So you know which way we'll be going then?"

Daggert felt unreasonably irritated with Sancho's defection, and the fact that she was talking to the dog instead of him.

"Thanks for saddling Lulubelle."

"Call her Belle. That other name is stupid for a horse."

"Noted," she said. "And I guess we won't talk about the fact that Enrique's riding Dandelion."

James tossed his cold coffee on the fire. "You'd better eat," he said, handing her a plate of eggs and grilled toast he'd kept warm for her.

"Please. I'm barely to the coffee stage."

"Give it to the dog, then," he said.

"You want some of these eggs, boy?"

He did. She scraped the contents of her plate on to a flat rock.

"His name is Sancho."

Sancho inhaled the food she'd set out for him, and wagged his tail at her.

"Apt," she said. "Every Don Quixote needs a Sancho, right, boy?"

Daggert didn't know which he disliked more, the
ice queen with her barbed tongue or this falsely smiling tourist. And the damnable truth was he wanted to
kiss her either way.

"I think we're going to have to set a couple of
ground rules," she said, making his hackles rise. "I
realize that I know nothing about tracking and that's
why you're here. At the same time, you know nothing
about Enrique, and that's why I'm here. I see no reason we can't work together harmoniously."

Daggert stood up. He'd known the pretty smiles
and the butter-wouldn't-melt-in-her-mouth routine
was a sham, but darned if he hadn't fallen for it, anyway.

He quickly rubbed their plates with sand, wiped
them with paper napkins, which he tossed into the
dying flames, and stowed them in one of his saddlebags. He poured the remaining coffee on the fire and
folded the pot in a heat-resistant cloth, shoving it in
with the plates.

He rerolled her sleeping bag into a tight bolster—
the woman had obviously never camped a day in her
pampered life—and secured it to the back of Belle's
saddle. He tossed handfuls of sand on to the remaining coals and scuffed more on to them with his boot.

She rose and dusted her jeans.

"We're heading north," he said, bending over and
cupping his hands to give her a leg up.

"That's the spirit," she said, stepping into his
hand. She put all her weight into it, instead of using
it as a hoist. He tossed her upward, and she landed
in the saddle with a low "Oof."

"Thank you," she said, as if he'd merely given her a boost. "It's good to know we have a meeting of the minds here." Though she spoke cheerfully enough, he didn't meet her gaze.

He reached for her stirrups to lower them.

She shoved her boots into the footholds and pressed down. "I don't think so, Mr. Daggert. I may be forced to ride on a western monstrosity, but I refuse the full discomfort."

He decided that icy tone of voice fit her long, elegant body to a T.

"Suit yourself." She'd be singing a different tune by midday.

"All the children at Rancho Milagro keep a journal. It was one of my partner's ideas—a chance for the kids to download. I read Enrique's before we set out," she said. Her falsely cheerful note was back. Why did Daggert think her more dangerous when she used it?

He swung his leg over Stone's broad back.

"Have you ever heard of a place called Cima La Luz?"

"In the mountains," he said.

"Light Peak, right?"

He grunted an assent.

"I'm beginning to suspect you're not a morning person." When he didn't answer, she continued, "I believe Enrique might be heading there."

Daggert stared at her coldly. "You didn't think it important to tell me that yesterday?" he asked finally.

Her smile faltered but she didn't flinch. "You

didn't exactly give me a chance,'' she said. Her eyes
dared him to deny this.

"Lady, if you don't kill yourself riding like that, I
might just do it for you. Good thing we're heading
toward Cima La Luz or I'd flay you right now just
for the sheer hell of it. But just out of curiosity, why
didn't you tell me this yesterday?''

The flush that stained her cheeks gave him all the
answer he needed. She'd been testing him.

He spurred his horse forward while giving Sancho
a go-ahead whistle.

"I'm sorry," she called from behind him.

Daggert ground his teeth.

By the time the sun was directly overhead, the last
thought on Leeza's mind was cheerful needling. Her
fears for Enrique were escalating with each passing
hour. Her guilt was on the rise, as well. And her ir-
ritation with one noncommunicative tracker was boiling like mercury in a burning thermometer.

She'd tried giving him the same silent treatment
he'd accorded her. Unfortunately, that seemed to
work perfectly for him. She'd babbled at him and
he'd ridden ahead. She'd hidden her exhausted tears
from him the night before, and blinked them back
now, but doubted he'd care even if he did see them.

He didn't seem the slightest bit affected by the elements, the cruel sun, the cold morning or the fact
that Enrique had been missing for at least thirty-nine
hours now. In fact, Daggert seemed so indifferent to
his surroundings he might as well have been made
from bedrock, as she'd first imagined him to be.

And why she found herself attracted to him, she couldn't even begin to fathom. It must be a by-product of the worry she felt for Enrique, and the unfamiliarity of searching for a child who didn't want to be found.

It was the hostage syndrome, she thought, where a captive transferred feelings of faith to her abductor. Patty Hearst had done it; so had countless others.

Except Leeza wasn't a hostage, she'd come on this mission against the tracker's express wishes. She'd demanded to be included.

She was forced to admit he would have made better time without her. Any discomfort she felt was her own fault entirely.

Given her nature, this did not make her feel remotely better.

"He can use that chip on his shoulder to light a forest fire," she told Belle. She grinned, feeling a little giddy. "Okay, wait, I have another one. There once was a man named Daggert…that's too hard. There once was a man named James, who never would talk to the dames."

"Enjoying yourself?"

She blushed as she never had before. It wasn't a gentle rise of color; it was a raging conflagration of embarrassment. She hadn't seen him halt his horse, and had caught up with him, literally unaware. But she lifted her chin, met his eyes directly and said, "Immensely."

"We'll stop here for lunch," he said, and dismounted.

"Fine. Good." Her stomach growled at the mere

thought of food. She'd been foolish to give her eggs to Sancho. But she wasn't about to admit it. "Belle could use a break."

"Right," he said. "Want a hand down?"

"No, thank you. I'm perfectly capable."

"Just keep hold of the saddle horn."

It took her about five minutes to dismount and another five before she could let go of the saddle horn. "I'd kill him," she murmured to Belle, "but then how would we find Enrique? And I'm not sure I could find my way back alone."

She gratefully accepted the moist towelettes he handed her, and leaned against the large boulder he'd selected as a shady picnic spot. She'd been too tired—and too busy making up nasty Daggert limericks—to notice the terrain while riding. It had changed considerably since dawn.

Low foothills, sparsely covered with scrub pine and liberally dotted with cholla cactus and chamisa, gave way to taller mountains in the distance. She'd read somewhere, probably in the material that came when they were first considering buying Rancho Milagro, that the Guadalupe Mountains weren't technically part of the Rocky Mountains proper. They belonged to an older range, from the Devonian Period, and were more similar in nature to the Appalachians than to the Rockies, filled with caves, such as the Carlsbad Caverns, and pocketed with numerous sinkholes. Beneath the Guadalupes, oil awaited recovery, and within them somewhere, a little nine-year-old boy needed rescue.

Daggert whistled for Sancho and set out a bowl of water for him.

Leeza waited for a cup this time and accepted the warmish liquid with as much gratitude as she had the towelettes. She remained standing as she drank this time; however, her bottom being so sore she'd have cried out at contact with the solid ground.

Apparently unfazed by the long ride, Daggert sat down Indian-style and used a long, curved knife to pry apart something in a deep pouch. A moment later he pulled out a long strip of beef jerky. Using the blade of the knife, he handed the piece up to her.

While she was a personal fan of beef, believing recent medical findings declaring red meat to be rich in iron and calcium, she couldn't say she was remotely fond of it salted, dried and rendered into strips of peppered leather. Add jalapeños to it and it was pure torture.

She spat her bite into her used towelette.

Daggert used his knife to tear off another piece of jerky and tossed it to an eager Sancho.

Sancho caught the bit of beef with alacrity and gulped it down after slashing it only a couple of times with his white teeth. He sat on the pebbled sand and whined.

Daggert tossed him another piece, which the dog caught but set down. He whined again.

"What is it, boy?" Daggert asked.

The dog lifted his right paw as if wanting to shake hands, or as if he'd acquired a thorn.

Daggert checked the raised paw, apparently found

nothing amiss and ruffled the dog's neck. "Go ahead," he said.

The dog looked from the beef to his master and whined as he again lifted his paw.

"What are you telling me, Sancho-dog?" Daggert asked.

Sancho barked in answer before finally eating the piece of jerky he'd set aside.

Daggert watched him, frowning, then tore another piece free and passed it up to Leeza.

She held up her hand. "Please. No."

"Too hot?" he asked. "So you're as tender mouthed as you are a tenderfoot."

"I think I have this figured out," she said. "In your mind, I'm the 'disliked one,' the one who caused Enrique to run away."

Daggert looked at the dog nearby. He gave Sancho a nod and the setter answered with a swift bark before tearing away from the picnic site.

"You don't even want your dog to hear this," Leeza said.

Daggert sighed, and the patronizing patience on his face fanned her fury. "You've decided the whole subject is taboo—at least you won't talk to me about it. You don't care to know the reasons why he may have decided to dislike me. Not you. Oh, you asked me last night, but you didn't make any comment on my answer. Because you don't care. Your mind is made up. It's as obvious as the nose on your chiseled face that you're making me a whipping boy. The more discomfort I feel, the more you like it. And you think the harder you push me, the more I'll fall apart right in front of your golden eyes. Do you want to know why?''

He didn't say anything, but his eyes had narrowed.

''I do,'' she said, ignoring the sign of his growing anger. ''I've had hours to study the question. And I think I have the answer. I think your whipping-boy complex stems from a deep-rooted fury at yourself because you didn't manage to find someone. That you failed in your big search once. I don't know who or what they meant to you, but it was—''

Leeza didn't see Daggert move. She heard a low growl and a whoosh and then felt the wind being knocked out of her. For a full two seconds, she wasn't even aware he'd lunged at her.

She focused on several things simultaneously: his muscled body pressing her against the boulder behind her. The knife he'd been using to tear the beef jerky being held against the hollow of her throat. And the tawny eyes she'd stupidly thought unreadable glaring into hers, filled with rage.

''Never talk about my son again,'' he said. How had she thought his voice was like velvet? It was a razor, sharp and deadly.

She tried to nod, but his hand against her chin prevented movement.

So slowly it made her tremble, he lowered the knife's point from her throat. But he didn't release her. His eyes still burned with fury, but no longer, thankfully, with murderous intent. His knife hand trailed down her arm in a slow, strangely electrifying sensation. It was the very opposite of sensual, yet every nerve ending she possessed seemed attuned to his touch.

"Tell me you're listening to me," he growled.

"I—I'm listening."

"Tell me you won't do it again."

"I won't. Of course I won't." She could feel the heat of his body covering hers and sharp edges of the boulder digging into her shoulder blades. She registered the corded muscles in his legs against hers and, most of all, his arousal. "Please," she murmured, not sure what she was asking him for.

"Please?" he whispered.

Her breath felt trapped inside her and she was fairly sure he could feel her heart thundering against his chest. He looked from her eyes to her lips, and something twisted on his face. His eyes closed and she had to bite back a whimper as she felt the anger draining from him.

When he opened his eyes again, she realized that while the anger might be ebbing, the tension in him hadn't. But it was tension of another kind. A sort that met her head-on, man to woman.

"You have a smart mouth," he said.

As if answering for her, her lips parted of their own volition.

She knew he was going to kiss her, and knew she should protest. Wanted to protest. Ached to find the means to tell him that he should back off and leave her alone. Instead, she leaned into his lips, meeting him halfway.

His mouth was as hot as his anger had been, and every bit as ruthless. He plundered her lips with determined purpose, a roughly banked passion. His tongue warred with hers, demanding capitulation. He was liquid and solid all at the same time.

She heard the knife clatter to the base of the boulder, then felt his hands strafing her body. He'd used those same hands to gentle the horses, but on her, he incited a riot.

She'd imagined running her hands across his broad shoulders, down the rippling muscles of his back, and didn't know when she began doing so in reality. One moment she'd literally been as afraid as she'd ever been in her life, and the next she was matching his passion touch for touch, kiss for kiss.

His lips gentled and he uttered a low, pained groan. His hands on her body slowed, still exploring her curves, and somehow the new tenderness in his touch made her feel inexplicably confused. Passion she understood, at least to some degree. Tenderness she didn't understand at all; it had never been a part of her life.

Daggert raised a hand to her face and molded it gently as he kissed her. And she could taste his withdrawal.

He pulled back from her, his eyes once again unreadable, his emotions masked. He straightened and ever so slowly ran the back of his hand over his moistened lips, still gazing at her.

She remained sprawled against the rock, a discarded rag doll with heaving breasts and glassy blue eyes. And she knew desire was written all over her.

He bent and picked up his knife. He pressed a button and slowly folded the blade back into the handle. It seemed a metaphor, and perhaps was.

Chapter 4

Leeza Nelson, former boardroom wizard, watched James Daggert stomp away from the lunch campsite and disappear around a huge boulder much like the one she sprawled against.

She lifted a shaking hand to her lips, half expecting them to be different somehow.

They were. They seemed fuller, more sensitive. *Stunned.*

Her lips felt stunned.

She felt stunned.

She was a veritable thesaurus of shattered— shocked, aghast, astonished and utterly confounded.

She'd been pushing him, needling him, trying to goad him into talking to her. She'd been trying to get him to finally acknowledge her as more than a nuisance. She would have been content to have him yell at her, or fall apart at the proverbial seams in obvious frustration. Anything to get him to speak to her, instead of being a silent rock riding in front of her.

Of all the things she hated in life, the worst was being ignored. She'd made a career and an entire life out of being the person most noticed, most sought after, most desired. Ignored wasn't in her repertoire.

Until she'd begun this journey to search for Enrique.

But Daggert's reaction to her prodding wasn't what she'd expected. She would never have anticipated it in a million and one years.

In her high-rise office in Washington, D.C., she could dig at people with impunity; if they didn't want to deliver what she wanted to know, they might not receive the dollars they sought from her. Needling was a seemingly necessary evil, and her right.

In those instances, however, whoever came knocking at *her* door was playing with fire. This time, she'd been the one taunting the flame.

Never in her wildest thoughts had she imagined she would rip at him with such uncanny accuracy. Nor would she ever have dreamed that such an attack would bring him to the point of murder.

Her hand lowered to her throat. Where she'd envisioned blood, perhaps a permanent reminder of the lesson "don't play with fire," Daggert hadn't left so much as a mark. That he hadn't branded her didn't address his fury, but rather a measure of the icy control she'd glimpsed several times in the short while she'd spent following him in his search for Enrique.

But he'd demanded she never speak of his *son*. Not

a nameless someone he'd been hired to find, not a stranger—his son.

Leeza closed her eyes. She let her body be warmed by the heat within the boulder, the sun beating down on the arroyo, and her own embarrassment.

She didn't want to even think about what losing a child would do to a man's psyche, to his heart. If she was right in her analysis of his dramatic response, James Daggert had once searched for his own missing son and either had not found him or had not managed to find him alive. Either case must bring the worst possible pain to a parent. It explained so much about the unusual tracker.

"Oh, I'm so very sorry," she said aloud, and her voice seemed to echo in the narrow dry riverbed.

But Daggert wasn't there to hear her, and she wasn't apologizing for anything she'd done, but offering the absent man her heartfelt sympathy.

She'd lost her parents, a grief she still felt with every passing day. He'd lost his *son.* His *child.*

She forced herself from the boulder and stood, albeit shakily. The world hadn't slipped on its very axis, as she felt it should have. The sun still beat straight down on the narrow, boulder-strewn arroyo, and the sand beneath her feet remained hot and slippery. The sky was still blue and the yellow chamisa bushes still smelled like skunks.

Daggert's horse, Stone, pulled at some threads of grass on the bank about thirty feet away and whispered something to Belle. The mare nickered back.

Everything seemed normal, yet nothing was. Nor could it ever be again.

Enrique was missing. Had been for hours upon hours. Leeza knew she had lost him by pushing him too hard. And she was literally shaking in her boots, not wholly from guilt, not entirely from remorse, and not even in horror at Daggert's furious response. She shook in a stunned reaction to his kiss.

A *kiss*.

"Just a kiss," she said aloud.

Belle whickered.

"Okay, so it seemed like a lot more than a kiss."

Stone gave a grunt.

"All right, a whole lot more than a kiss."

Neither horse answered vocally, but Stone shook his head, his reddish-brown mane dancing in the air.

Leeza cautiously approached Belle and withdrew a notebook from her saddlebag, then her cell phone from the pommel, which Westerners aptly called a saddle horn.

Retreating to a different boulder, she penned her confusion in the notebook, jotting down her fears, her wishes about the next twenty-four hours. Never once did she mention her gigging James Daggert. Nor did she describe the kiss.

And she didn't fill the rest of the notebook with her response to that kiss, as she could have.

Some things were better left unsaid.

When James Daggert hadn't returned an hour later, Leeza broke down and tried some of the beef jerky from the pouch he'd discarded earlier. It still burned her tongue and made her stomach roil, but she knew the man was right about needing to keep up her strength, and she wasn't about to dig in his saddlebags in search of something else to eat. If words could set off his fury, what might violating his privacy do? She was tempted, but didn't want to bring on a confrontation.

After eating the vile jerky, she tried calling the ranch on her cell phone again. She couldn't even reach an operator. All she heard was a scratchy message telling her she was out of range in an undefined area.

What else was new?

She tidied up the site and, more as an apology than from any real sense of the saddle being uncomfortable, fumbled with the buckles and straps to lower the stirrups two full notches. She led Belle to the side of the boulder where Daggert had kissed her so thoroughly.

"I'm going to mount now," she announced grimly. "You move so much as a step away and I'll send you to a knackery when we get back to the ranch."

The horse rolled her eyes.

"Believe me, they'll probably love rendering you. And if they don't, I will."

Belle grunted but remained placid.

With the stirrups lowered, and by climbing up on the boulder, Leeza was able to get astride Belle without Daggert's helping hands. It wasn't that she didn't want to touch the man; it was that she wanted to do precisely that. And have him do the same to her. And more.

And she wanted to tell him she was sorry for goading him.

What she didn't want to do, much as she ached to

know the story, was to ask-him about his son. That would have to come from him, if and when he ever decided to forgive her or to confide in her.

But she wasn't about to be the supplicant. She would never beg for absolution. At least, the Leeza Nelson who used to live inside her body as recently as three days before would never have begged. This Leeza now, the one who had left everything she knew behind to follow a stranger into the mountains on a search for a lonely little boy—*she* might just have a few pleas tucked away.

She only had to wait astride her horse for a few minutes before James Daggert came back into view.

Her heart leaped at the sight of him and she felt every inch a fool. The man was just a man, and rude, at that. So he'd kissed her. What did that mean in the grand scheme of things?

Nothing.

Everything.

"Nothing," she muttered aloud.

Daggert checked his stride and his tawny eyes traveled from her head to her feet.

Leeza thought his gaze would move up again in that age-old macho affirmation and condemnation some men could manage with a single, melting look.

But James Daggert's gaze locked on her lowered stirrups.

His eyes shifted away before meeting hers. The passion still lingered on his face, as did some anger, but she couldn't tell if the latter was directed at her or at himself.

He didn't provide an explanation for his hour-long

absence. He merely swung a leg over Stone's back
and settled into the saddle. Without a word, he urged
the horse forward. And without a backward glance,
he headed away from the narrow escarpment he'd
chosen for their lunch break.

Leeza followed, angry at his dismissal of her, but
not trying to get him to speak now. She wouldn't have
known what to say to him, and would have bitten her
tongue off before attempting an apology to his rigid
back.

Watching his broad shoulders up ahead, Leeza
wondered what motivated the man. She suspected she
now understood at least some of the demons that tor-
mented him, but what kept him so focused on tracking? She'd seen people with lesser trouble crumble
and abandon their professions, dreams and desires.
Even having lost his son, Daggert kept pursuing the
misplaced children of the world. Why? How could
he, when doing so had to bring back every memory,
every torment each time he mounted a search?

Though he hated to halt for a second night, afraid
the boy's chances decreased with every delay, Daggert had to rein in Stone and whistle for Sancho when
the shadows lengthened and the sun dipped low on
the western horizon.

Now that they were higher into the foothills, darkness would come swiftly and bring with it the first
taste of winter. September in New Mexico always felt
tumultuous—one day hotter than hell, the next pro-
ducing a surprise snowfall. Nights could dip below

freezing and sunny days could burn the leaves off trees before they even turned to gold.

But weather wasn't the worst he feared could befall the little runaway. Being out-of-doors and alone wasn't bad, not really bad. There were far more terrible horrors out here in these mountains.

When Daggert had left the woman earlier, shock at his own actions sending him on a long, soul-searching walk, he'd found tracks belonging to Enrique's horse—that telltale bent horseshoe nail. Though he'd searched, he hadn't found tracks of another horse, one not shod by the Milagro farrier.

While this filled him with relief, he hadn't been able to shake the neck-tickling sensation that someone else was out in these mountains watching every move the boy made, and Daggert literally ached to keep going.

It's someone Donny knew.

Someone *he* knew. *The butcher, the baker, the candlestick maker...*

But they had to stop for the night. If he was tired— and God knew he was—the woman had to be worn to her very bones.

Daggert glanced back at Leeza Nelson. She'd already halted her horse and was working at dismounting.

She hadn't said a single thing to him all afternoon. Guilt stabbed him.

The lady's muscles weren't cooperating with her efforts to get off her horse, and she seemed scarcely aware of her surroundings. If he hadn't known how sore she must be, he might have found the scene vaguely humorous.

But he did know, and he also knew just how enormous an apology he owed her.

He moved Stone back to flank Belle.

"Here," he said. "Hand me her reins."

Though she looked at him without understanding, she did as he asked.

"Shake free of your stirrups. That's right. Roll your feet at the ankle. Good. Now, put your arms around my neck and hold on."

She hesitated.

"Trust me," he said.

To her credit, she didn't slant one of her patented "Oh, *right,*" looks at him. But she didn't move either, except to sway a bit.

He sighed. "It's okay," he said. "I know I haven't given you any reason to, but trust me. Come on, Leeza."

He held out his free hand.

She looked at it as if he might strike her with it.

She might as well have stabbed him with his own knife. "Leeza. Trust me. Please. Put your arms around me. I wouldn't let you fall."

He suspected his use of her name compelled her to lift her arms. He felt the warmth of her sun-gilded shirt and her struggle not to place any weight against him.

He reached for her waist and felt her stiffen, leaning away from him. "Trust me."

"I'm so confused," she said, and he knew it was true. He also suspected that trust didn't come easily to Leeza Nelson, though why he felt so certain about this, he couldn't have said. It was simply a fact, like her beauty.

Her body leaned into his, and Daggert could feel how she ached with wanting even if he wasn't certain it wasn't his own desire projecting on to her.

"Hold on tight," he said, but he should have warned himself to hold on. A part of him, alive for the first time in several years, needed to be very careful.

"One, two, three." In one sure move, he hoisted her out of her saddle and on to his lap, where he sat astride Stone.

As she had the evening before, Leeza startled him by limply nestling against him, her exhaustion stripping her of all defenses. Remembering her statements in the firelight, he was sure she'd be surprised to learn that vulnerability was an incredibly alluring quality in a human, especially in one as strong and lovely as Leeza Nelson.

He wrapped his arms around her.

"I'm so sorry," she said.

Thinking she was apologizing for her physical weakness, he said, "It's okay."

"I'm not sorry about this," she said, and raised one of her tired hands to the base of his neck. As she had from the very first moment he saw her, she surprised him. He would never have expected this powerful woman to admit to any physical frailty, to concede to exhaustion.

As her fingers curled into his hair, he felt a spear of true desire drive through him.

"I'm not, either," he said honestly.

"I'm sorry for what I said to you earlier."

He waited for her to say more. She didn't, and he wondered at that. In the first place, she owed him no apology. In the second, most people attempted to mount a defense of their actions, their words. *I didn't want to hurt you, but…* or *I'm sorry, but you made me so…* Leeza Nelson felt she owed him an apology, but not an explanation.

Hers was a straightforward acknowledgment of fault or guilt, with no groundwork laid for self-exculpation. And all the while her fingertips lay quiescent at the base of his neck, as if they felt the very pulse of him beating, throbbing.

As the silence stretched, with him trying to form words of apology himself, Stone stomped a foot as if prodding him along. How did one go about saying he was sorry for having held her at knifepoint?

Finally, Daggert said, "What I did was damnable." Like her, he wouldn't give an explanation, but he owed her more than a handful of words. Much more. "I—"

"I'm not sorry about the kiss," she interrupted, her cheek pressed against his chest.

Fierce desire stabbed at him.

He closed his eyes. "Me, either," he admitted.

"Will we do it again, do you think?"

His eyes flew open and he felt he was seeing a wholly new landscape. A brighter one. A sharper one. He smiled. "Lady, you can take it to the bank."

She chuckled.

The feel of her weak laughter against him was both

an erotic sensation and one so strangely intimate that he felt arousal shifting to something more complex and disturbing.

If Stone hadn't stomped his foot again, Daggert might have sat there all night, holding her against him, his senses filled with the scent of her hair, the texture of silk against his lips.

"Hang on," he said, and clasped her to him, hiking her up. He swung his leg over Stone's neck, holding Belle's reins with one hand and Leeza's waist with the other. He shook his foot free of the stirrup and gently dropped the two of them to the ground.

Leeza slid down his body, leaning against him as she regained her land legs. Her silken wisps of hair tickled his chin and her hands clung to his shoulders. Without looking at him, she said, "I would never have admitted this, but I owe you one. The stirrups felt better lowered."

Daggert couldn't help it. He laughed aloud.

Stone sidled a couple of steps away from them, apparently as startled by the unfamiliar sound as his rider.

Daggert looked down at Leeza and found her studying him with an unreadable expression on her lovely face.

"What?" he couldn't help asking.

"You should laugh more often."

"Because?"

"Because it takes my breath away when you do," she said, efficiently stealing his.

Knowing it was wrong, but unable to resist the temptation of her parted lips, Daggert slowly lowered his mouth to hers. The universe seemed to shrink to this one point of connection, her lips drawing him closer, her tongue teasing his. She tasted of possibility, and kissing her was like discovering that hope and promise could still exist somewhere.

Chapter 5

Leeza felt his kiss to the very depths of her soul. She didn't understand this man, didn't understand what was happening to her, but she knew she didn't want this new awareness of emotions to stop.

When he pulled away from her, looking at her for a moment with such raw need that it made her knees seem to turn to liquid, she'd wanted to cling to him, to pull him back to her.

Instead, she let him go. In her lifetime of dealing with people, she'd never encountered anyone she couldn't read, couldn't understand. James Daggert was the very first.

And this terrified her in a way she couldn't name.

The fear she felt about him had nothing whatsoever in common with the fear she felt for little Enrique.

For the boy, she worried about rattlesnakes, bears, mountain lions or even starvation.

About Daggert, she feared a tearing asunder of her very orderly universe.

Leeza had accepted the currycomb from Daggert and was working the dust free from Belle's rough coat. "That's ridiculous," she told Belle as she brushed the mare down. Leeza had expected the task to be wearying, but instead, it relaxed her own taxed body.

Belle made a whinnying sound, but her muscles began to lose their rigidity.

Leeza felt a moment of pride that she'd managed to accomplish such a relatively simple job.

By the time she'd finished brushing her horse, Daggert had concluded his own therapeutic session with Stone and was already setting up their night's camp.

Without a word, Leeza started gathering wood and rocks for their fire. With a single appraising look, Daggert left her to the task and began to fashion long hackamores—hand-crocheted rope ties that looped around the horses' heads and noses without slipping between their teeth—in lieu of the bridles they'd worn for two full days.

Leeza listened as he talked to the horses as if they were long-time friends. His words were inconsequential, the meaning nominal, but the low, gentle voice acted on her as powerfully as it did on the horses, making her muscles unknot, her shoulders lose tension and pain. She'd heard of horse whisperers, but never that they had such an effect on people.

Daggert loosely tethered the beasts to a low branch

on a much larger scrub oak than he'd found the night before. "Eat this good grass," he told them. "Then you can have some oats for dessert."

Both horses bent their heads to the tall, plentiful mountain grass as if completely understanding him.

Though as thoroughly exhausted as she had been the night before, Leeza didn't succumb to tears, finding it much easier—and safer—to busy herself with the small tasks of heating water for the pouches of food Daggert housed in his saddlebags, and hopefully demonstrating she wasn't a total loss as a tracker's assistant.

She'd seen the distrust in his eyes that first day. And every minute after that. And she'd seen the wanting in them there, too. But desire was cheap and she craved far more than that.

She needed his help to find Enrique, but she *wanted* his respect.

It had been a long time since she'd felt the need to prove herself, to have to work for esteem. She reined supreme in her world, her position hard won and carefully preserved. Out in this wilderness, with worry and fear nibbling at her every second, ineptitude a stumbling block, and an unfamiliar sense of connection with this unusual man scattering her normally acute mind into utter chaos, she found she needed him to want her on this mission with him.

She told herself that some of this came from the darkest part of her childhood, that because she'd always been regarded as a rescued orphan, she'd wound up with some sort of provider complex.

But she knew that a larger measure of it came from

beginning to seriously respect James Daggert's opinion. Discounting her unfortunate words, her reaction to his kisses—their kisses—she realized she no longer viewed him as a hired guide, but as a man. A man who could help her locate a missing child. Help her find Enrique Dominguez.

Daggert's dog, Sancho, came racing into camp, carrying something black in his mouth, his brown coat covered with burrs and dried grass. Leeza's heart jolted when she recognized what he carried, and her fingers shook as she removed one of Enrique's gloves from the dog's teeth.

"Daggert," she called.

The man materialized beside her and took the glove from her nerveless fingers. "This the boy's?"

She nodded, and found herself pressing her hands against her mouth to keep from assaulting the man with questions.

"This is a good sign," he said.

Her hands fell from her mouth. "How can you say that?" she asked, irrationally furious with him for being so calm.

"He lost it in the heat of the day, didn't even notice it. We started out twelve hours behind him, and Sancho brought this in *tonight*. That means we're not that far behind him now."

His tawny eyes met hers squarely. *Trust me.*

Her fury dissipated as swiftly as it had risen. "Really? You're not just saying this to make me feel better?"

He gave her a look she interpreted as meaning such a thought had never crossed his mind. For some unknown reason, instead of angering her, this particular expression pleased her. It could only mean he was telling nothing but the absolute truth.

She asked, "Then shouldn't we keep going?"

He shook his head. "Too dangerous. Even if it had risen early, the moon's not quite full enough to provide enough light, and the horses could stumble. It's a wonder the boy got so far the first night. He must be a pretty good rider. Anyone else we'd have caught up to earlier today. Still, he's been going steadily slower with each passing hour."

Frustration nipped at Leeza, trying to get her to ignore the dangers and push on.

"Relax," Daggert said. "The boy will stop, too. His horse will make him."

"What makes you think so?"

"He didn't bring water for his horse, and no oats. The horse will demand a rest. He's leading the boy to water. They're probably camping on the bank of a river up ahead right now."

"If he's okay."

Daggert held up the glove and turned it over. "No blood. No scratches. The only marks on it are from Sancho's teeth. The boy just dropped it. People who are hurt don't drop things, they abandon them, and whatever happened to them usually shows."

Leeza drew a deep breath, as grateful for Daggert's calm now as she'd been angry with him for it before. She searched his face, trying to see if he was telling her everything. She suspected he wasn't, but she could also read a measure of relief on his features.

Sancho's bringing Enrique's glove had made him relax for some unknown reason.

She leaned down and petted the animal. "You are the most amazing dog in the world," she said.

She poured him some water.

Sancho grinned at her before slurping up the liquid, stretching, then dropping his finely shaped head on Daggert's saddle. The very fact that the dog was lying down, waiting for his dinner, forced her to accept the fact that Daggert was telling the truth and there was nothing more they could do that night.

Within minutes, the fire popped and crackled. Sparks shot into the nearly pitch-black sky; flames danced in the rapidly cooling breeze. Sitting beside the circle of stones, Leeza knew the sight should have warmed her, but it didn't; Enrique had been missing now for some forty-five hours.

She was barely surviving the journey. How could a little boy who'd taken some tortillas, peanut butter, a container of milk and a bag of cookies possibly be faring after forty hours? Especially with only one glove on a cold September night.

A small moan escaped her.

"What makes you think Enrique's going to Cima La Luz?" Daggert asked, bringing her attention back to their warm campsite. And how did he always seem to know exactly what she was thinking? To her certain knowledge, no one had ever been able to read her before.

She'd faced down dozens of young sharks at boardroom tables. When she was younger, a baby in the venture capital game, they'd eyed her like a tasty treat they were prepared to devour. Later, when she'd become the head shark, they'd swum around her very cautiously, even obsequiously. But no one had ever been able to read her.

He handed her a plate of beef stroganoff that smelled surprisingly delicious. He nodded at her. "Cima La Luz?" he prompted.

"The other night, when I was showing him the constellations, he told me his parents were up there. I thought he meant in heaven."

"You don't think so now?"

"Yes—I mean, yes, they're certainly deceased. But I don't think Enrique is accepting this. I think he meant somewhere specific. In his journal... Corrie makes all the children keep journals. Supposedly they can download all their anguish on to the pages and become healthy."

Daggert gave a half smile. "You don't believe it works?"

She hesitated, then shrugged, thinking about her own notebook jottings. "Anyway, there were all sorts of references to this Cima La Luz. He seemed to think it a place where spaceships land and take or bring back abductees. I know it sounds crazy—"

"Not so crazy. People have been seeing weird lights at the Cima for years."

Leeza wasn't struck so much by the news of unusual lights on a mountaintop as she was by the sheer magic of actually conversing with James Daggert.

"So little Enrique believes his parents were abducted by aliens?"

"I'm afraid so," she said. He'd called the boy "little Enrique.'' What did that say about the man? That he cared? That he felt something about the child he sought? That he was reminded of his own lost son?

''What happened to his parents?'' he asked.

''They were apparently killed in a skirmish with a very real bad guy calling himself *El Patron.*''

''Apparently?''

Leeza made a face, ''According to Chance Salazar, one of my partners' husbands—''

''I know him,'' Daggert said, but he didn't elaborate. Leeza couldn't tell from his tone if the knowledge was good or bad.

''Chance said this *El Patron* compelled people to do things for him by holding family members hostage. And if they refused, he would either kill the hostage or have the people killed outright.''

''And that's what happened to Enrique's parents?''

''Police think so. They didn't find them, but they disappeared, and there was enough DNA evidence in *El Patron*'s garden to include them in another charge of murder against him.''

''And Enrique escaped?''

''He was with his aunt in Mexico when it happened. She couldn't keep him, which is how he came to be with us.''

''And now he thinks his parents weren't killed at all, but abducted by aliens.''

''Denial can be an attractive piece of real estate,'' she said.

Daggert gave her an odd look, one both measuring and slightly rueful, but he said, ''True. Reality's ground is much stonier.''

She gave him a shallow smile instead of doing a double take, as she wanted to. He'd followed her thoughts so completely that she felt off balance.

She sampled the stroganoff. Not quite as tasty as the primavera, but certainly edible. Within seconds, she'd cleared her plate and momentarily envied Sancho's freedom to lick his dish. Nodding at the dog, she asked, "Why do you give him a different dinner than we have?"

Daggert smiled slowly. "He doesn't ask for seconds this way. If I give him the same thing I eat, he's convinced he'll be able to con me out of half of mine. Since he's usually right, I give him something else."

She scrubbed her plate with sand, as she'd seen Daggert do the night before, and wiped it clean with a dry napkin. She did the same for Daggert's and Sancho's, still slightly amazed that the procedure did such a thorough job.

It wasn't until Daggert poured them each a cup of hot coffee that the tension between them seemed to come back full force. She'd been hiding behind the routine camp tasks to avoid thinking, and talking with him had allayed her fears.

But now, with their stomachs full, the night fully black and stars once again beating down on them, she was assaulted by the awareness that she was alone with this man, a man she wanted, a stranger with chasms of conflicting emotions hiding just beneath the surface.

Despite the night's chill, the warmth from the fire apparently prompted Daggert to roll back his sleeves to his elbows. He performed the task with the slow deliberation he applied to everything, and Leeza found herself mesmerized by the movements of his hands.

She noticed abrasions on his wrist. "What happened there?" she asked.

He gave her a questioning look, then followed her gaze to his wrist. "It's nothing," he said.

"I've got some cream in my bag," she said, and rose to retrieve it.

"Don't bother," he said. "I'm fine."

She didn't stop. She rummaged in her pack, found the narrow tube of Neosporin cream and went back to sit beside him. She concentrated on opening the tube and squeezing a bit of the thick cream on to her fingertip.

She motioned for him to present his wrist. He did with a shadowed expression on his face, his eyes unreadable, though they flickered with reflections of the fire.

She smeared the cream on to the abrasions. "When did this happen?" she asked.

"I looped the horses' reins over my wrist. Belle stepped sideways. No big deal."

Leeza vaguely remembered his jerking back when he'd been carrying her from Belle the day before. She wasn't sure what to think about the fact that he'd been injured while helping her, no matter how much he considered it insignificant.

She smoothed the cream in, aware of little else but the velvet feel of his skin beneath her fingertip.

He moved his wrist out of her reach and she felt as if he broke a spell. She was glad the shadows would hide a blush from him. She tossed the tube of antibacterial cream into her bag and picked up her coffee. The silence between them felt heavier than it had before.

Daggert sighed as if he'd lost an argument with himself. When he spoke, she knew what the internal war had been about. "My son Donny was a couple of years younger than Enrique when he disappeared," Daggert said. He sipped at his coffee, not looking at her.

Everything in Leeza grew still, waiting for him to continue. She wanted to hear the story, and dreaded what she might learn about the man who told it.

"That was four years ago. He'd be eleven now. Not even a teenager yet." Daggert clenched his hand around his coffee cup hard enough to bend the aluminum. "He'd been over at a friend's house. It wasn't far. He'd walked the path home with me at least a hundred times."

Leeza wanted to close her eyes against the sight of Daggert's face flickering in the golden firelight. A sorrow too deep for words clouded his features, darkened his eyes.

People who worked with her believed she had a heart of stone, or made bets on whether she possessed one at all. She'd heard the jokes about the head of the corporation who couldn't feel for an employee because she had a hole where her heart was supposed to be.

She'd always known she had the hole, and maybe a heart. She just hadn't felt it twinge before. Not until Enrique. She felt it wrench now with Daggert talking about his little boy. *Oh, please let this be a happy ending,* she begged silently, even as she knew from his earlier anger that it couldn't be.

"I'd persuaded Alma not to worry about him. That he was a big boy and a little walk alone was good for him. She believed me. Sometimes I've been angry with her for that."

Even as Leeza wondered who Alma was, Daggert startled her by tossing his coffee into the flames. The fire sputtered furiously for a moment and sent sparks spiraling. "Donny never came home," he said starkly.

Daggert poured another cup of the hot coffee and set the pot back on the rocks. Leeza suspected he'd all but forgotten she sat there beside him, needing to hear the rest of his terrible story, fearful of its conclusion.

"I found him." His eyes flicked to hers. "That's what I do, find people." He looked away. "But I found him too late."

Leeza closed her eyes, unable to continue to watch the muscle working in Daggert's tense jaw. She ached to reach out and just touch him, a humanistic stroke of compassion, but somehow knew he needed to get through this revelation without hindrance.

"He hadn't run away. He wasn't lost. He was stolen. A madman took my little boy and killed him. And left him cold and alone in these mountains."

"Dear God," Leeza said, opening her eyes.

"I'm not telling you this to scare you about finding Enrique. I'll find him. I swear to you I will. I'm telling you this because…'' Daggert didn't finish his thought, just stared into the flames. ''Damn,'' he said.

When he didn't say anything for what seemed an eon, she prompted, ''Because?''

''Because I held a knife on you today.''

A knife? He'd kissed her. That was the bigger issue. The main trouble. ''It's okay,'' she said swiftly. ''I understand.''

''No,'' he said sharply, his eyes cutting to hers. ''It's not okay, and no, you don't understand. I'll bet everyone told you that I'm one of the best trackers around. But I'll bet they didn't tell you that I've always got a hidden agenda. You can't know that I'll never stop searching for the man who hurt Donny, and you can't know what that means. You don't know that the anger in me is always there. *Always.* I wake up with it. I eat with it, sleep with it. It's the most real part of me.''

And as he spoke, she could see it. Feel it radiating out from him. The fire jumped as if it were fueled by it.

Leeza shook her head, not negating what he was saying—who was she to argue with what motivated James Daggert?—but denying that it was the most real part of him.

''Vengeance is mine…'' she murmured.

His eyes burned into hers. ''Sayeth the Lord? Save it. Vengeance *is* mine. You want to call it justice? My people would call it avenging Donny's death. Call it by any name and it's the same to me. The man who stole my son, the man who killed my boy, that man deserves to die," he said roughly. "And I'm the man who's going to kill him."

When she didn't say anything—couldn't say anything—he continued. "It's a fact. And this fact burns anyone I come in contact with."

The fire in front of them crackled and sent a spark toward Daggert. He waved it away as he might a stray insect. "It drove my wife away. My friends. Or rather, I drove them off."

Leeza knew he was trying to warn her, telling her that she could be burned by this rage ablaze in him.

She'd tasted it. The passion, the fury. The pain. And survived.

So far. "And so you continue searching for lost children," she said calmly, relieved that the night hid her trembling from him.

"And the man who stole Donny, who stole others."

"What others?"

"Over the past ten years? Fifteen of them."

"*Fifteen!* And no one's told me about this?"

"Most people don't believe it's the same person. Some are called accidents. Others, animal attacks."

"But you think it's a serial killer." And she didn't make it a question because she knew that he didn't think of it as one. For James Daggert, there was no room for doubt. His was a world of absolutes. Blacks and whites.

And hers?

A world of numbers—reds and blacks.

"Yes. A serial killer." He sounded almost relieved at her prosaic statement.

"Tell me," she said.

"A hiker. A housewife on an afternoon stroll. A couple out to neck in the woods. Donny. A kid who went hang-gliding. Others. Some were mauled like Donny was. Authorities claim it was a mountain lion. A rogue."

"They were all killed this way?"

"No. They claim the hiker just fell."

"They?"

"The authorities. Your partner's husband, others like him."

She understood Daggert's flat tone when talking about Chance Salazar now. "But you don't believe this?" she asked.

"No."

"Why?"

"Because there was another set of tracks on the ledge above the point where they discovered the hiker's body," he said.

"And the others?"

"The housewife was like Donny, just out for an afternoon stroll, and she never came home. I found her about two weeks later. The authorities called it an animal attack."

"But you don't believe that?"

He gave what might have been called a ghost of a chuckle, except there was nothing humorous in his demeanor. "That same rogue? No. They even called in the Forest Service animal control. One of the men told me later the body was clawed by a mountain lion, all right, but not one like anyone's ever encountered before."

"Doesn't that prove the rogue theory?"

"No," Daggert said tersely.

Leeza waited, hugging her arms to her body.

"It wasn't like any lion because the claw marks were anomalous, running in patterns and directions a lion wouldn't make unless thoroughly enraged. As in rabid or worse. And beside that obvious fact, the point was moot. Cats—all cats, big or small—have what they call living claws. They shed DNA all over the place. This one didn't. It was dead."

"I don't understand," Leeza said, fighting the gooseflesh prickling her skin at his words.

"A live lion doesn't have 'dead' claws. The matter they found wasn't from a live lion, but from one that was long dead. They even found a few stray hairs from the fur. And some lint." He stopped speaking for a while, then said, with a shake of his head, "Lint."

Leeza asked, "And this wasn't enough to launch an investigation?"

"The Forest Service guy was only one man on a team and no one seemed to think his findings very important. What's discovered in a test tube couldn't hold up against what they could see with their eyes."

Leeza remembered the Rancho Milagro housekeeper, Rita, talking about warm El Niño winds and the monster they brought with them to the Carlsbad. A monster who stole children and ripped at them with sharp *chubacabra* claws.

In the superstitious world according to Rita, this myth explained the very real disappearances of several children over the last ten years. It had taken a private and pointed reprimand from Leeza to make her stop. The children had taken the stories in stride— except for ceasing to play outside at night—but the tales had made Leeza acutely aware of the remote location of the ranch, the isolation, and most of all, her own sense of inadequacy as one of the house-mothers.

"What's a *chubacabra?*" she asked Daggert now.

He gave her an wryly sympathetic look. "A story to scare children with. Nothing more. Whatever killed Donny wasn't some mythological goatsucker."

"It's a goatsucker? What's that?"

"Not the birds, that's for sure. In truth, it's nothing. A myth. There's no such thing as a *chubacabra.* Just a tale."

"So you believe whatever hurt your son was a man."

"Flesh and blood, yes. A man? No, he's a monster."

She hated to ask the question, but had to. "Do you think this man could have Enrique?"

Daggert shook his head. "I've been watching for other footprints, other hoofprints. Nothing. So far, the boy is alone." He didn't have to spell out for her what might happen if the child did run afoul of this monster, and she clamped her mind shut on her too vivid imagination.

"So you think he's okay tonight?"

Daggert didn't answer and she realized he didn't need to. He couldn't possibly know for certain what had befallen Enrique. All they knew was that the boy was missing a glove and had tossed away gum wrappers.

Leeza said, "He doesn't fit any pattern. He ran away."

"He ran away, but into what?"

"He just ran away. Please. It's simple." Why had she said "please"? Did she want him to stop, to keep a truth from her? She was the one who always needed every piece of data, refusing to embark on a venture unless every detail was laid before her.

"Nothing's simple," Daggert said.

Leeza felt something inside twisting into a tight knot. "Say there was such a thing as a cat with 'dead' claws, would you believe in the mountain lion theory then?" she asked.

"No. Because a big cat seldom comes into town. Even if one did, a big cat won't drag its prey forty miles."

"Forty miles!"

"Donny went missing in Carlsbad. I found him on Cima La Luz."

"Oh my God," Leeza said, instinctively reaching out to Daggert and touching his forearm. "I'm so sorry." A muscle jumped beneath her fingers and she withdrew her hand sharply.

She couldn't imagine how difficult this trek must be for James Daggert—following the same path he'd followed to find his own son's mangled body.

Finally, she asked, "And that's your life?"

"My life?"

"Vengeance. Justice. That's your life?"

"Yes. It's enough for me," he said with bleak finality. Then, without looking at her, he added, "We better get some sleep."

Sleep was the furthest thing from her mind. But she could accept his changing the subject. "I never asked what people call you," she said.

"Pinnéniqua."

"What?"

"It's Apache."

"That's your name? Your Apache name?" She thought how she'd imagined he looked every bit an Indian warrior with the hard planes of his face and his jet-black long hair.

He gave a half smile, but there was nothing remotely friendly about it.

"What does it mean? And how do you say it again?"

"Pin-né-ni-qua. It means Bitter Man Who Walks with Ghosts."

Leeza blinked. A man searching for and finding his own son too late would be a bitter man indeed. "Your parents gave you that name when you were born?"

Daggert's smile warmed slightly. "No. Donny's mother did, after he was gone."

"Pin-né—what?"

"Call me Daggert or James. It doesn't matter."

Somehow, she thought it might. He'd been the one to offer the information about his Indian name. She remembered something that Pablo, one of the ranch hands, had mentioned before she and the tracker set out on this trek. He'd said that Daggert didn't talk much to outsiders. She'd taken it as a slur against her eastern lineage, but now suspected Pablo had been referring to James Daggert's Apache heritage.

Leeza wanted to reach out to him, not just physically, but emotionally, as well. She wanted to acknowledge the enormity of his confidence. Her friends and partners, Jeannie and Corrie, the fellow orphans she'd met in college and bonded with like none other, were the only people she ever allowed inside, the only ones who truly knew her. With them, she didn't have to pick over possible segues; she just knew how to talk, how to be open. With this man, with the tragedy in his past still so present in his haunted eyes, she didn't have a clue how to go about sharing a facet of herself in exchange.

"Do you need some help?" he asked.

Startled, she raised her gaze and met the full force of his unusual eyes. Though they had been sitting side-by-side during the entire aftermath of dinner, somehow he seemed closer now. Close enough to feel the warmth of his breath.

"Getting into those shiny red pajamas," he drawled.

She was sure she was every bit as red as the material of her sleepwear. "No, thank you, Mr. Daggert. I—I think I can manage."

He leaned closer and lifted a hand to her chin, stroking her skin with a callused thumb. She felt the touch to her very soul.

"I can be a very good assistant," he murmured against her bare throat.

She moaned a little and let her head fall back to allow him greater access.

"If I were to give you an Apache name," he said, pulling her blouse open slightly and pressing his lips to the ridges of her collarbone, "I would call you *Denzhoné Bidáá.*"

Despite the catch in her breath, she asked him to repeat it, thinking that the man's soft voice might have been created to speak the Apache phrase. He complied. It sounded slurred and silken, more of a hum than distinct syllables.

"What does it mean?" she breathed.

He kissed her instead of answering. His lips, warm and firm, captured hers and plied them gently, tenderly. Questingly.

The fire paled by the comparison to the blaze he lit in her. She gave a small moan of acceptance, of undiluted pleasure, and leaned into the caress, into his hands. The kiss deepened, ripened into full passion. Because he was less conflicted this time, Daggert's mouth was hot with desire only, with a hunger pure and unfettered, uncomplicated and sincere.

As he slid them lower to the ground, cushioning her head with one hand while slowly caressing her with the other, she found herself losing touch with the night, with worry, with everything but the feel of this man's growing fervor. And her own.

Sancho barked and, abruptly, she was alone.

Daggert, as if telekinetic, stood some five feet from her, on the other side of the fire, one hand holding his opened knife and the other splayed, ready for a fight. His legs were bent slightly and his head tilted to one side.

Sancho growled.

Leeza struggled to regain a seating position, still breathing raggedly from his kisses. Her eyes strafed the black countryside, frantically trying to ascertain what lurked outside the light of the campfire. "What is it?" she asked.

Daggert waved his free hand, hushing her.

A coyote howled somewhere very close. The peculiar yipping sounds sent chills down her spine and splashed gooseflesh across her skin. She must have made some noise, for both Daggert and Sancho turned cold eyes in her direction.

The coyote gave another call, which was echoed by another farther away.

Daggert bent to the fire, his knife tucked away and his tension reined in. He added more of the wood she'd gathered earlier. "Another lost pup," he said. "That's his mother calling him home."

"Coyote, right?"

Daggert lifted his eyes in her direction and smiled a little. The shadows played across the hard features, softening them. "Don't worry. I won't let them get you, *Denzhoné*."

She couldn't remember anyone ever giving her a name before. Perhaps her parents had had pet names for her when she was a little girl, but she couldn't remember any if they had. And John and Cora Nelson didn't believe in such nonsense.

Leeza gave him a slightly tremulous smile. "I'll hold you to that," she said.

"We'd better turn in," he said.

She felt a pang of regret even as she let her breath out in a sigh of relief. It was better to face the reality of the cold night than to give in to the bliss of the amnesiac quality of his kisses. She could lose herself in his arms and then who would worry about Enrique?

Worse, who would save her from emotions she'd never encountered before and didn't know how to handle?

Conscious of the coyotes so close to camp, she asked Daggert to walk with her to their rough toilet facilities and to turn his back as he had the night before. She told herself not to feel self-conscious, but did nevertheless.

As she swiftly prepared for bed, donning her pajamas, she noticed that this time he didn't burn himself.

But when she turned around she could feel his gaze on every inch of her. And her red satin pajamas might as well have been transparent.

"Does *Denzhoné* mean 'red'?" she asked suspiciously.

"No." He didn't elaborate.

"What does it mean, then?" she asked.

He slid his hand into her hair and pulled her to him. The kiss was no less tender, no less filled with carefully banked passion, but it also carried a note of finality.

"Good night, *Denzhoné Bidáá.*"

"You're not going to tell me, are you?" she asked, a slight smile on her lips.

"Not tonight."

"And why is that?"

"Because you'd seduce me and we'd get a late start in the morning."

She was still smiling as she pulled the flap of her sleeping bag up to her chin.

The stars didn't seem quite as heavy that night and she found herself relaxing into the rhythm of Daggert's slow and steady breathing. She stretched a hand out of her sleeping bag and tucked it into his curled palm. His breathing never changed, but his fingers tightened around hers.

Sometime in the middle of the night she dreamed she heard him singing softly, and when she turned to look at him, he'd turned into a black wolf. The Daggert wolf stared at her for a long time, then, at some little sound in the darkness, turned and disappeared into the dark.

She heard him call out her name with a long low howl.

But the howl was lonely and filled with despair.

In a fireless camp, halfway between the site where Daggert and Leeza slept, and the place where the boy they sought huddled beneath a tall pine tree standing beside a narrow sliver of a tributary that would lead to the Rio Grande, the hunter played with his toys. A serrated hunting knife with an intricately hand-carved hilt, a pair of preserved mountain lion claws, a bear claw, a map. He set them on the blanket in front of him, scarcely able to see them in the darkness he needed to remain invisible. He didn't have to look at them; touch alone gave him great pleasure.

A coyote howled in the distance and the hunter

smiled. The woman and the boy would be frightened. They were on their way to learning their lessons.

And when he was finished with them, Daggert would learn his.

The hunter chuckled aloud.

Chapter 6

Leeza was up with Daggert, working beside him in the cold predawn. She fed the horses as he prepared the human breakfasts. She ate her meal with the same alacrity Sancho displayed. She sand-washed the plates afterward while Daggert rolled the sleeping bags.

"You're a quick study," he said.

As compliments went, it was moderately banal, but it suffused her with pride. It told her she was learning to hold her own even in the remote wilds of New Mexico.

"Thank you," she said. "In another eon or two, I might just get the knack of this. How are you at financials?"

"I've never heard that word in the plural before, so I'd hazard a guess I would be lousy at it," Daggert said.

Leeza chuckled. His response was so silly it was funny. And so simple it had to be genuine. Hard core real. Her laughter evaporated. He'd never heard *financial* in the plural before. What did that tell her? That he didn't play the stock market? That he didn't have a mind? That he didn't have a portfolio with a tracker's retirement safely tucked away in some 401K drawer?

It told her that in his world, perhaps the real world, such things didn't matter. That they suddenly didn't matter to her so much anymore was troubling.

And strangely freeing.

"We'd better hit the road," he said.

"Fine," she answered. She felt stiff and was relatively certain that if this trek lasted much longer she would discover a whole new meaning of discomfort.

Still, she felt eager to move out. If Daggert was right and Enrique wasn't far ahead of them, they could possibly find the boy by lunchtime and be heading back to Rancho Milagro shortly thereafter.

Daggert's meticulous attention to breaking camp was vaguely annoying, as it seemed to take precious time. Enrique had been out in this wilderness for some fifty-eight hours now.

Finally, Daggert turned and offered her a leg up onto Belle. Leeza all but flew onto the saddle. He helped position her stirrups, and Leeza's heart literally skipped a beat. His hand on her calf made her feel like a schoolgirl in the midst of her first slow dance. When he ran that same hand up her jeans and rested it on her thigh, she couldn't breathe.

"We'll find him," he said. "Don't worry."

She felt a stab of guilt that she hadn't even been thinking of Enrique. Not with Daggert's hands on her. It was all she could do to stay on the horse and not slide down into his arms.

He patted her leg and turned to mount Stone. A few seconds earlier, she hadn't wanted to waste a single moment of time, needing to find Enrique. Now, perversely, a part of her wanted to stay right where they were, and test the proverbial waters of their mutual desire for each other.

Even as she thought it, she realized he'd ridden out of their campsite, leaving her to catch up. As they rode higher and higher into the mountains, she caught the heady scent of pine, felt the chill of rising above five thousand feet, and heard the raucous calls of the Stellar's jays, the black-hooded mountain birds commonly called camp robbers. She relieved the pressure on her rear by standing in the stirrups. She often witnessed Daggert doing the same.

Her cell phone worked for a few precious minutes along about midmorning, as they came out on top of a rocky ridge. No one at the ranch had heard a thing from Enrique. Chance Salazar's men had checked all bus stations and airports from Carlsbad to Roswell, and none of the employees at any of them had seen a little boy fitting Enrique's description.

Leeza told Jeannie about Sancho bringing in one of Enrique's gloves and Daggert's analysis of what that might mean. Jeannie told her that some of the townspeople had also gone looking for Enrique. "It's a big wilderness. They know Daggert's the best in the business, but they're worried about a boy being out there so long. Mr. Jenkins from one of the grocery stores in Carlsbad. Jack, Chance's former deputy. Bill, the manager of Annie's Café. They're all up there, in the mountains, too.''

Jeannie was cut off while assuring Leeza that their collective faith lay in the two tracking Enrique into the mountains. ''Just be careful, honey. People say Daggert's—''

''He's what?'' Leeza had called out. ''What about Daggert?''

She grimaced at the static-filled cell phone. It had been fully charged before she'd started on the trek, and she had an extra battery pack in her saddlebags, but she'd never dreamed the mission would take longer than a couple of days at most. But it wasn't batteries that caused the static; once again she was simply out of range.

''They haven't seen him,'' Leeza said.

''As long as the horse hasn't come back to the barn without him, we're okay,'' Daggert said. ''And even then, we'd have Sancho to smell him out.''

Surprising her, Daggert smiled. She couldn't help but smile back.

''That's better. As you told me, you should do that more often,'' he said. ''The river's up ahead and we'll stop there for lunch.''

Leeza wondered at Daggert's seeking her smile. She smiled easily and often. At least, with Jeannie and Corrie. She'd never thought about her smile before. There wasn't too much to smile about in venture speculation, except when a deal worked or a new business galloped toward earning a slot on the stock exchange. And she wasn't one to fraternize with her staff or other corporate sharks.

She'd been stunned at the rich sound of Daggert's laughter and hadn't lied to him when she'd told him it literally stole her breath. Now he'd told her she should smile more often. Did her smile have the same effect on him that his laughter did on her?

The mere notion brought a smile to her lips, and suddenly her heart felt lighter than it had in days. The hope that they would soon find Enrique buoyed her spirits every bit as much as did considering what it would take to make Daggert laugh again.

Though they traveled for an additional few hours, it seemed to take mere minutes to descend a long escarpment leading to the river Daggert had said would be there. Despite the slippery bed of pine needles underfoot, the horses stepped livelier the nearer they came to fresh water. Leeza understood exactly how they felt.

"What's the name of this river?" she asked.

Daggert shook his head. "It's just a tributary. It's one of a hundred feeders for the Rio Grande. This one's bigger than some, smaller than others. I call it Rio Cima, because it's on this mountain."

She thought about that as she held the horses' reins, letting them drink their fill in the gurgling, clear brook Daggert called a river. By comparison, the Potomac seemed an ocean.

His words had seemed so prosaic and yet the meaning behind them somehow prophetic. It was similar, in a way, to those life statements her adoptive parents had fed her throughout her childhood years. Only

Daggert's assessment of the tributaries threw everything into a tight perspective. Some troubles were bigger than others, some smaller. It was a remarkably simple way of dividing complexities.

Could she begin to use this paradigm to explain how she felt about this unusual man? That some of her feelings about him were stronger, some conflicted?

Daggert whistled for Sancho and wandered away, kneeling beneath one pine, then another. He studied the ground and searched the low-hanging branches before coming back to join her.

"I'm starving," he said, reaching into his saddlebags and pulling out three of his magic food pouches. "I want a real meal. While I'm getting the fire going, why don't you take a dip in the river? It'll be colder than hell, but…" He shrugged.

"You're sure we can spare the time?" Leeza asked, eyeing the water wistfully.

"See that tree over there?"

"Yes?"

"Enrique slept under it last night. I'm guessing we're only a few hours behind him."

"Footprints?"

"Right. And hoofprints. The ranch's farrier always turns one nail backward. It's as distinctive as signing a portrait."

"And Enrique wears Nikes."

Daggert grinned. "Did I say you're a quick study? More like greased lightning."

Leeza smiled and was rewarded with a quick flick of his forefinger across her cheek. She felt the smile on her face slipping as reaction shot through her. It was just a touch. A careless, yet intensely intimate touch.

"Enjoy your bath," he said.

"Oh, I can promise you I will," Leeza said, summoning her voice, her smile.

She relinquished the horses' reins to him and quickly removed a small backpack from one of Belle's saddlebags. She was behind a stand of trees flanking the river before he could tie the horses to a branch near some thick, tasty-looking grass.

She stripped out of her clothes with more speed than grace and decided not to pussyfoot getting into the water. She grabbed a washcloth, aimed for a clear, quiet section of the river, turned her back on it and allowed herself to fall backward, landing in the icy water with an enormous splash. She was on her feet in less than a nanosecond, gasping for air and giving a short shriek of pure shock.

Daggert materialized on the shore, poised for rescue, ready to fight whatever had made her scream. A saddlebag dangled from his hand. He slowly straightened.

Leeza couldn't move. The ridiculously small washcloth she held in her hand wouldn't cover much more than the wedge of blond hair at the apex of her legs.

She'd never been wholly naked with a fully dressed man before. It made her feel strangely galvanized and shy simultaneously. Her heart thundered in her chest. *Come to me,* she pleaded silently.

Daggert's eyes caressed her, touching the puckered aureoles and the hardened nipples of her breasts, slipping down her flat belly and lower, lingering there as the heat rose in him. She could see him swell, could feel the heat in his gaze. His eyes continued down the length of her legs and seemed to pierce the water that lapped about her knees.

And as he studied her, he dropped the saddlebags and began slowly removing his clothes.

A frisson of pure heat swept over her and she felt her legs tremble.

He never took his eyes from her as he dropped each article of clothing to the grassy slope above the river.

His body proved to be tanned all over, and with a jolt Leeza realized it was no tan but his natural skin color, a warm earth tone. Every inch of him was as beautiful as his voice. Broad shoulders winged out over muscled arms; tiny dark nipples were the only adornment to his smooth, hairless chest. Well-defined abdominal muscles tapered past his waist, and the muscles in his thighs rippled as he moved forward.

He was fully aroused, and the sheer evidence made a molten river rush to Leeza's core. She moistened her trembling lips with the tip of her tongue and knew she would soon taste him instead. She shivered, not from the river's chill but from undiluted anticipation.

He seemed impervious to the icy cold of the water or the sharp stones on the bed beneath. He came slowly, steadily, inexorably toward her—three or four steps that seemed to take forever. With every gliding movement, Leeza's breath came more raggedly, and her knees wanted to buckle.

She could feel the heat radiating from Daggert, as if he was feverish. And when he stopped inches from her, she felt as though he were a magnet and she the metal pulled to him. She rocked a little, the river pushing her, the feel of him drawing her. When he touched her, a single fingertip to a rock-hard nipple, she gave a half sob of pure longing. He slid his hands across her face and into her hair and drew her to him for a kiss filled with such raw hunger that she felt as if she might explode with the echoing need. But the heat in his mouth, the velvet softness of his tongue, shaped the ache into passion that matched his in every way.

His hands lowered to her shoulders, her breasts, her waist. He stroked her, exploring every curve with a firm, sure touch. And all the while, his mouth plied hers, demanding, exhorting, giving and taking simultaneously.

His hands grasped her rounded bottom and kneaded gently, questingly, before pulling her sharply to him, letting her feel his arousal. She moaned and reached out to discover the secrets of his body. He drew his breath in with a sharp hiss when her cold, wet washcloth met the small of his back. Stepping back from her, he took the cloth from her unresisting hand, dipped it into the water and gave it a swift squeeze before lifting it to her breasts. She gasped as he ran the icy washcloth over her nipples, then followed with his hot mouth. He suckled and laved until she was cupping his head and arching into him.

Daggert caught her at the waist and lifted her out of the water into his arms. He carried her to the grassy bank and set her down. She could barely stand. He yanked open the saddlebag he'd dropped earlier and pulled out a Polartec blanket that he shook free and spread on the ground.

He took her hand and held it against his chest, sandwiching it between his heart and his hand. "*Denzhoné Bidáá*, come to my bed."

Leeza, mesmerized by his soft voice, his use of Apache, his body and the way he made hers feel, nodded and allowed him to pull her down to the blanket. It was warm and soft, and his body pressing against hers was hot and hard.

He ran the freezing washcloth across her belly and again chased the chill away with his heated tongue. He gently plied the cloth lower and kissed away its sting. He parted her legs and teased her with the cloth there as well. And with his mouth incited a riot.

She shouldn't be doing this, she thought chaotically. Every part of her screamed with need, while her mind raged against it. She shouldn't pause in her search for Enrique, but couldn't think about Enrique with Daggert's lips on her.

"James," she cried out as he found the very center of her and caressed her with his wicked tongue.

The combination of making love outdoors, her deep ache for him and his kissing her so intimately swept away all thought, focusing her awareness on one thing only: that single point beneath his lips. Her legs began to quiver and her body to contract. He continued to caress her, faster and deeper, then abruptly stopped, not taking his mouth from her body, but keeping perfectly still against her.

Leeza cried out in surprise as a primal orgasm as strong as any tsunami swept through her. It caught her unaware, unprepared, as relentless and pure as the most exquisite force of nature could be. She felt lost in it, ripped from the earth and hurled into some other plane of existence.

He encouraged her to ride the tidal wave, touching her, kissing her, then slowly soothing her, catching her effortlessly and bringing her back into this world from the other dimension he'd sent her to. He massaged her belly, kissed her heaving breasts, nuzzled each nipple with thorough attention. She clung to his shoulders and blinked back tears of sheer release.

He raised himself over her, curtaining her with his long, black hair which smelled of sunshine and the man himself. Leeza took in his glittering gaze of need. She lifted her hands to his face and stroked the long hair from his smooth cheeks and angular jaw.

He caught her fingertips with his lips and sucked at them gently.

"Come inside me," she murmured. "Please." She opened her legs to him and felt him throbbing against her.

He hesitated.

Heedless of consequences, she took the decision from him by wrapping her legs around him, impaling herself with his shaft and sheathing him with her liquid warmth.

"*Denzhoné*," he growled, his jaw clenched, his face contorted with what looked like stunning pain as he filled her.

He sank into her dewy body, encased by her, enfolded into her warmth, her honeyed core, her silken skin. She took him fully, expanding to fit him within her, gasping as he drove deeply and slowly into her.

Daggert could feel her tightly holding him, her elegant long legs around his back, her inner muscles clenching and imploring him. Her lips lifted to his and she echoed her movements with her mouth, drawing his tongue inside and sucking softly.

A moan of pleasure escaped her and unlocked the control he'd been exercising to keep from plundering her. Leaning on his forearms to avoid crushing her, he covered her breasts with his hands, molding them with his fingers as he rocked into her, thrusting, penetrating, losing himself in her incredible body.

He still had enough awareness left to know that what they were doing was dangerous. Aside from physical considerations, he knew she didn't understand that his heart was irrevocably committed to his search for Donny's killer. He knew this, knew the pitfalls it created, and still relished the wonder of her beneath him, in his arms.

"James Daggert," she murmured, arching up to meet his thrusts, pushing her firm breasts deeper into his hands.

He left her lips to suckle her turgid nipples as he arched and drove into her with even more force. She gasped and thrust upward, joining him with a need as great as his own. Clasping her to him, holding her shoulders, he drove ever deeper, ramming into her with an almost desperate urgency.

She cried out, inchoate in her desire. Suddenly she clenched around him, her inner muscles squeezing, contracting, drawing him inevitably over the edge.

He arched suddenly, calling her name as he released into her, and his shuddering explosion propelled her into another climax as well. She gasped and shook beneath him, around him, with him.

He felt barriers dropping inside him. If kissing her had tasted like promise and possibility, making love to her felt like the very essence of hope.

She'd matched him stroke for touch. She'd accepted everything he had offered and had given herself readily and without games.

Tears trailed down her temples now, dampening her hair.

"Why are you crying?" he asked, stroking away the tears, the sight of them chiseling away at his heart.

She shook her head. "It was just so beautiful. So perfect."

He smiled a little. "And this makes you cry?"

"It's never happened before."

He stilled. "What hasn't?"

She opened her eyes and met his. Though he'd been calling her "Beautiful Eyes" for the past day and a half, he'd never seen anything quite as luminous as hers were now.

"I used to think there was something wrong with me," she said. "I even asked my friends about it. They didn't know what to tell me."

"I don't understand," Daggert said, stroking her face, caressing her skin, still buried in her and wanting even more.

Color stole into her cheeks, but her eyes didn't waver. "I didn't know making love could feel so...so wonderful. Thank you.'' A tear snaked toward her hair and he caught it with his finger.

The tear—tangible evidence of emotions she wouldn't reveal beyond their union—glittered in the sunlight and seemed to burn him every bit as much as her thanking him did.

This woman had followed him into the hills, into the mountains, not knowing at all what to expect. She'd been totally out of her element. And for much of their journey, he'd treated her like an extra saddle-bag on an already packed horse.

He'd only lightened up a bit today, lying about being hungry, knowing she couldn't handle jalapeño-doused beef jerky again and that, without food, she wouldn't make it through another day. Figuring she would relish a dip in the stream, he'd persuaded her to try the cold waters of the river, and had forced himself to close a door against the thought of her naked body.

And he'd managed it until she screamed.

He'd run for her, as he'd run for no one else besides his family before. He'd pictured Donny's killer with a knife at her throat, mountain cat claws tearing the flesh from her body.

Daggert hadn't even been aware he was still holding one of the saddlebags in his hand until he saw her.

She should have looked like a drowned rat, spent and frozen stiff.

But she hadn't looked that way at all. She'd looked a lot like Venus rising out of that shell. Instead of copious amounts of flowing titian hair, Leeza's short locks had been plastered to her head, turning the golden silk to a tawny-brown as river water trickled down her incredible body.

But she'd been every bit as naked as Botticelli's *Venus*.

And beautiful in a way that had robbed Daggert of speech.

Naked as the day she was born, but filled out and all woman.

It would have taken one of the miracles Rancho Milagro doled out with such alacrity to make him turn back to fixing their lunch.

If she'd told him to leave, he might have. If she'd ordered him to turn his back, he probably could have done so. But she'd stood there gazing at him, and nothing on God's green earth could have stopped him from wanting her.

And he wanted her still, even knowing he had nothing to offer this woman who had everything, this woman who didn't even know how easily she pierced a man's heart. If he still had a claim to his heart, he would gladly give it to her, lay it at her feet and beg her to be his forever.

But his heart wasn't his to give. He'd exchanged it for the power to find Donny's killer. And that was all he had room for in that place in his chest. The place that used to hold compassion, hope, faith and trust.

She made him want those things, and wanting them felt like a betrayal of his vow to Donny. Daggert couldn't feel anything until the day that his son was truly avenged, that the truth of his death was revealed for all to see.

Couldn't she sense that?

Perhaps she could. She hadn't asked anything of him, hadn't sought affirmation or commitment.

She'd said she'd never experienced anything so wonderful before. Until now. Until him.

This made him feel like a god. A Pure-D, amazing god.

And it shamed him because he had nothing more than incredible chemistry to offer this lovely woman. He could find the boy she sought. He could do a thousand little things that might make her ice princess heart yearn for his, but the end result would always be the same: he had no room for anything but finding the man who'd killed his son.

"I was adopted," she said.

He felt the sun on his back, the soft blanket beneath his legs, her satin skin against his, and her words made him feel off-kilter, as if the world had slipped sideways. But he couldn't say anything.

"When I was nine."

He gently kissed the hollow of her collarbone.

"I was so scared," she said, and he could hear the fear still lurking in the little girl inside her. "I felt purchased. Paid for. Felt that if I screwed up, I would be turned out into the streets, a problem no more, abandoned like some people dispose of unwanted pets. I didn't screw up. Not that I would have been allowed to. In the world according to John and Cora Nelson, making mistakes indicates imprecise thinking, the worst indictment they could imagine."

"Did you love them?" Daggert asked, and wondered that the word could even be ripped from his mouth.

She frowned. "Love them? I don't know."

"Where are they now?"

"Out of my life," she said, and her flat tone of voice as she uttered the phrase told him more than a thousand impassioned statements might have. Whatever she felt about them wasn't resolved, any more than whatever she felt for little Enrique could be categorized easily.

Daggert felt he had to give her something. A gift beyond the one that left him feeling a god, because she'd appreciated it so.

He shifted away from her somewhat, and felt a frisson of desire when her muscles clenched around him as if she was wordlessly trying to keep him with her. He pressed his lips to the spot just below her full breasts, then said against her satin skin, "Roll over, *Denzhoné.*"

Making him smile, she languorously did as he asked. He frowned when he noticed the shadow of a bruise at the base of her beautiful, well-rounded bottom. He kissed the faint strip of purple. She sighed.

He began to slowly, carefully knead her overworked muscles, beginning with her shoulders and neck, massaging away the knots and the tensions of the past couple of days. He murmured to her in Apache, telling her how lovely she was, how soft her skin, how incredible her eyes and how perfect the hollow at the very base of her spine.

She was asleep before he finished, her body relaxed, a faint smile on her lips.

He spread his hands over her back like a shaman psychically exploring hidden pain. ''If I could give you anything, *Denzhoné,* I'd give you back your faith in your heart, the heart those cold people stole from you.''

He felt her give a silent sigh, and saw her fingers twitch slightly as if accepting his gift in her dream. And for some reason, he felt like crying.

The hunter petted Daggert's dog and shook hands with him as he always did whenever they met. The setter whined, as he always did.

Soon he would tie the dog to a tree—he wouldn't hurt the animal; he would have to be a monster to hurt a good dog—and leave him with a piece of the boy's clothing. He'd found a discarded child's glove only that morning and knew Daggert had already found the mate, if Sancho hadn't brought it to him between his white teeth.

Daggert would be frantic to find his dog. The hunter chuckled aloud, picturing the tracker's dismay when he discovered that his worst nightmare was two steps ahead of him.

The boy was only a couple hours up the mountain from him and Daggert and Leeza Nelson just a few hours behind. He had to slow them both if the lesson he wanted them to learn was to be of any amusement. They would be feeling safe now, sure of finding the boy, and they would be careless. And the loss of the ever-faithful Sancho would confuse the tracker.

The hunter fingered the mountain lion claws in his pack. He smoothed the dried-out fur, as lifeless now as the beast itself. But the claws were every bit as deadly as they'd ever been, and better because they no longer retracted.

He'd corral the boy first, leave something to terrify Leeza Nelson and put the fear of the devil into Daggert's half-breed heart, then proceed to make the boy understand the rules. Rules of survival, of boundaries; simple rules of life. And death.

Chapter 7

"We should go," Daggert said, stowing the cleaned and empty plates into his saddlebags.

Leeza nodded, unable to look at him. He'd given her more that afternoon than any man before him ever had. And she didn't understand it or know how to accept it. It wasn't just the physical glory he'd given her, but his words and the honesty in his granite face and heated eyes. And what had she given him in return? A pathetic tale about her childhood and a few moments' respite from a search that had to torment him.

"Sancho didn't come in," she said, unable to voice any of her confusion.

"He will," Daggert said, dusting off his jeans before tightening the cinch on one of the saddles.

"What if he's found Enrique?"

''Then he'll let us know.''

''How did you train him?''

''It wasn't really training. We work together,'' Daggert said.

''Like you and Stone.''

''Like that, yes.'' Daggert kicked out the small fire he'd made to heat their lunch. He cupped his hands to help her up onto Belle. ''You're working with Belle now, too.''

As she swung her leg over her mount's long tail, she realized that what he said was true in a way. When she'd started on this trek—was it only two days ago?—she'd distrusted the horse, considering her more a wicked beast than a helpmate. Yet not once had Belle failed her. A patient animal, she'd suffered a novice rider and undoubtedly inexplicable commands on her gentle mouth, and still hadn't spooked at any strange sounds, rustlings in the grass, nor had she tried ridding herself of the tired woman on her back.

They had become a team, this woman from the east and this horse from the west.

And she and Daggert? Wasn't there a parallel there, as well? She hadn't trusted the tracker beyond the obvious reliance on his skills. When had that changed? When he'd pulled her from her horse that first day? When he'd kissed her? When he'd told her about his son? She didn't know. She only knew that she did trust him. With her life. With Enrique's.

What did that mean? What could it mean in the future, the days beyond finding Enrique? Dare she even give such a thought consideration—that there might actually be a time when Enrique was safe and sound, and she and Daggert could see each other as an ordinary man and woman getting to know one another? Somehow that seemed impossible.

As it was impossible that she trusted Daggert now.

Except for Jeannie and Corrie, she didn't trust anyone. Never had and had firmly believed she never would.

Yet here she was in a mountain wilderness, trusting a man she had absolutely nothing in common with.

That thought made her pause. Were they really so dissimilar? Daggert was used to getting his own way. So was she. He was dedicated to his task. So was she. He was aloof and seemingly cold. Was she? Of course she was. There were more people who were scared of her than who appreciated her, let alone liked her.

Daggert had said he'd driven everyone away from him, turned them away. Hadn't she done the same thing over the years? Driven to succeed, to rise to the very top of the venture capital game, had she ever taken time to lend someone a helping hand along the way? She realized that if she asked anyone who had ever worked with her such a question, he or she would likely try to hide a snicker. "Leeza Nelson" and "consideration" wouldn't have been lumped together in any sentence.

She hadn't even offered a little, lonely boy comfort on a chilly night when he'd missed his parents.

Revenge drove Daggert; a need to prove herself drove Leeza. The motivations weren't the same, but they obviously produced some of the same results.

They left him alone and single-minded. Left her the same.

Did that make them a team?

No, but it made them natural allies in a sad sort of way.

And when this journey was over—when Enrique was back at Rancho Milagro, drawing pictures, grounded until his late thirties and telling the other children about his great adventure—Daggert would be pursuing Donny's killer, and she... Would she go back to being the Leeza Nelson she'd always been?

Three hours later, with the sun dipping toward the western horizon, Daggert barked a command for Stone to stop. He whistled again for Sancho, something he'd done several times in the past few hours.

No brown blur sprang from the horizon.

Surprising her, Daggert abruptly swung from his saddle with lithe grace.

Leeza's heart jumped into her throat. *Enrique.*

She didn't want to see what drew Daggert's attention, afraid it would be the broken body of a little boy. A little boy she so desperately wanted to draw into her arms and hold tightly. *Too little, too late. Please don't let it be too late.*

While she refused to let her eyes drop to the ground, she followed every hard line of Daggert's stiffening form. That something was terribly amiss was evident in his stance. The tension seizing the tracker was palpable, and Leeza found herself holding a hand over her mouth to keep in a keening cry of horror.

Stone whickered to Belle as if he understood his rider's motives. Belle sidled nervously.

Daggert slowly began to circle away from his horse. He'd gone about thirty yards when he stopped abruptly and knelt down, resting on his boot heels. But nothing about him was relaxed.

Even at that distance, Leeza could feel the tracker's worry. Her own heart rate accelerated as she watched Daggert staring down at the earth in front of him.

"What is it?" she called finally, summoning the courage to look at the ground, and not seeing the broken body she was so terrified of discovering lying there.

When he didn't answer, she slid from Belle's back and took up both horses' reins. She dragged them forward, her impatience to find out what Daggert had found at making her forget her general apprehension of horses. "Come on," she muttered.

The pair followed her as she crossed the clearing.

Daggert held out a hand to hold her back.

"What is it?"

He jutted his chin at a small wooden box lying in a patch of green grass among the pine needles. The box was small, roughly four inches long and some three inches high.

Daggert pulled out a handkerchief and shook it open. He used it to gingerly lift the box, and pried the lid open with his knife.

"What's in it?" she asked.

He held it out for her to see. It was a staggeringly lovely silver knife hilt, with an elaborate lightning bolt zigzagging down its length. The lightning was inlaid with turquoise and obsidian.

Still using the handkerchief, Daggert pried the hilt free from its case and depressed a small button hidden in the inlay. A curved knife blade with a signature etched in the carbon stainless steel sprang into position. The blade was serrated and obviously deadly.

It was no less beautiful now that it was revealed as a weapon. But it had a dark beauty, as if the knife had been tempered with evil and polished with a cloth of foul intention.

"What's wrong?" she asked, knowing only that something had to be, for James Daggert was literally shaking. Anger, despair, a grief too deep to be expressed all warred for supremacy on his rugged face.

"We're not alone on this mountain," he said, and the words were so softly spoken that they might have been casual thoughts. "Donny's killer is here."

Adrenaline shot through her. "Your son's killer?"

"The man who stole Donny, the man who killed my son, used a knife just like this one. Perhaps this very knife. This serrated edge has a unique pattern. And see the lightning bolt on the handle? This symbol was carved on the tree above Donny's...body. Your partner's husband, Chance, wasn't marshal back then. Jack was a deputy marshal, though. He believed Donny must have carved it himself. I knew better, but Jack wouldn't listen. He found Donny's little pocket knife open on the ground and pointed to that as evidence that Donny carved it. Hell, that little blade wouldn't have carved the crust off toast much less a lightning bolt in a spot a full foot higher than Donny could even reach.''

Leeza took this in and, after a hard struggle, forced herself to think about the present. "How can you know this box hasn't been out here for years?"

Again Daggert jutted his chin toward the spot where the knife had been lying. "The grass isn't disturbed, see?"

"Yes, but—"

"If it had been here even a day or so, the grass beneath would have withered or turned yellow. If the box had been here for years, it would have discolored, too. The grass isn't yellow at all, and see? It's already springing back, losing the imprint of the box. No, the knife's been here only a few hours at most."

"But someone else could have a knife like this," Leeza suggested hopefully. "Jeannie told me there are others out looking for Enrique. It could have been one of them."

"It's possible," Daggert agreed, lifting haggard eyes to hers. "But this is a custom-made knife. Even the presentation box is hand-carved, see? Something like this would cost almost a thousand dollars. No, it's the same man. I know it. I feel it."

He slid the lid back on the box, keeping it wrapped in his handkerchief. "He's between us and Enrique."

"What?"

"Enrique camped there beneath the trees where we…where we had lunch. Remember? I pointed it out. He tied his horse to that big pine on the riverbank." Daggert gestured back the way they'd come. "Didn't you see traces of the fire he tried to start?

The wood was wet. I'm surprised we didn't see smoke last night, but his campfire probably didn't burn long enough for us to glimpse it.''

Daggert was standing with his hand on the saddle-bag, his gaze turned inward, when suddenly he whirled on her. ''What did you say about others searching? Who? Who are the others?''

Startled by the abruptness of the question and the sharp note of urgency in his voice, Leeza blinked. She couldn't remember the names Jeannie had given her. She said as much to Daggert.

''Think, damn it. You know.''

''I am thinking,'' she snapped back. ''It didn't seem important to me, and I usually don't pay much attention to things if they're not of obvious importance.''

''Everything's important about this. Think, *Denzhoné*. Did she mention professions? Are they law enforcement? What? Butcher, baker, candlestick maker?''

At his prompting, Jeannie's words began to filter through Leeza's memory. She felt foolish, having so quickly forgotten. ''One of them is the man you mentioned—Jack, Chance's former deputy. He's retired, I think.''

Daggert's eyes narrowed. ''Jack.'' He said the name with a note of despair in his voice. ''It frustrated me when he couldn't see what was so obvious to me, but I never thought ill of him. Suspected he might be responsible.'' And his tone let Leeza know that Daggert would die another death if it proved that Jack was the madman who'd murdered his son. ''He's been a deputy marshal for years, a man who would do anything for someone he cares about.''

"One of them is a grocer—I don't remember his name. Another manages Annie's Café.''

"Anyone else?''

"No, I'm sure it was just those she mentioned.''

"A grocer—that could be John Jenkins or Tommy Gonzales. Or if you really stretched it to include a convenience store, Jordy Greathouse. God, this is a nightmare. And Bill Thompkins manages Annie's. I've known them all for most of my adult life.''

"Shouldn't we be going?'' Leeza asked, aching to stop Daggert's obvious torment and eager to find Enrique before their mysterious adversary did.

Daggert handed her the pretty box wrapped in his handkerchief. "Stow this in your saddlebag,'' he said.

Leeza took the deadly object from his hand, not asking why he was leaving it in her care. He was keeping it wrapped for possible fingerprinting later, but was giving it to her because he planned on ditching her at some point in the near future. She knew this with as much certainty as she knew the sun would rise in the morning and go down at night.

Once she'd safely secured the package in her bag, he asked, "Can you manage?''

Her heart leaped. He wasn't leaving her. "Of course,'' she said swiftly.

"Good. Then do whatever business you have to over there behind those trees and we'll head out.''

"Where's Sancho? Shouldn't he be here by now?'' Leeza asked, and wished she'd kept silent when Daggert's frown of worry intensified.

But all he said was, "He'll find us on the trail."

Leeza quickly made use of the sheltering trees and was back in the saddle again within minutes.

Daggert pushed the horses a bit faster, cutting through the thick foliage with such nervous energy and scarcely checked fury that Leeza felt her own nerves stretched to the breaking point. Every noise, every rustle seemed to harbor an evil that hadn't existed before.

On the journey thus far, she'd worried that Enrique might have fallen from his horse and be lying somewhere with a broken arm or a bump on his head or else covered in cactus needles. She'd pictured him cold, frightened and lonely. She'd never allowed herself to consider greater dangers.

She'd even managed to squelch fears of mountain lions or bears as soon as they entered her mind. When Daggert had told her what happened to Donny, she'd ruthlessly thrust away any correlation to Enrique. As she'd told Daggert, denial was an attractive piece of real estate and she'd readily taken up residence.

With the discovery of the knife Daggert recognized, with the awareness that someone was traveling between little Enrique and the people who desperately sought him, with the host of emotions playing on Daggert's face, Leeza was suddenly, sharply aware that a danger the likes of which she'd never encountered lurked just out of sight.

Every shadow hid a madman creeping behind pine and scrub oak. Her skin prickled with the feel of his murderous eyes upon her.

''Please, let us find Enrique safe,'' she whispered. And in her heart, she could hear the plea echoed, and another added to it: *Please let me have a second chance.*

Chapter 8

*T*he hunter caught up with the boy shortly before darkness blanketed the mountains.

The boy was wary of him, but not scared. He'd met him before, had accepted a stick of candy from him on at least two different occasions. All the children did. Some of the adults, too. There were no rules about not accepting candy from people you know.

"A lot of folks are out looking for you, son," the hunter said.

The boy appeared mulish, the way children did when they knew they were doing something wrong but intended to do it anyway. Lessons upon lessons.

"Where are you heading?"

"Are you going to stop me?" the boy asked.

"Maybe I'm here to help you."

"My parents are coming for me. They'll help me."

The hunter was interested. He knew for a fact that the boy's parents were dead. The days when he'd worked for El Patron *had been good ones, days filled with adventure and purpose.*

He asked the boy, "How are they going to find you out here?"

"They just know," the child said. He looked bedraggled and tired.

"Tell you what, boy, I'm as hungry as a bear after a long winter's nap and could use some grub. Care to share a picnic with me? And then we'll decide what to do about finding your folks."

The boy studied him with acute distrust for a long minute—something he'd have to pay for later—then asked, "Are you gonna light a fire?"

"Why, you cold?"

"Yes, but I don't want anybody to see the fire. There was a lot of smoke when I tried one."

You're telling me, the hunter thought. If Daggert hadn't been so blinded by the Nelson woman's red pajamas, he'd have seen the smoke himself. "Well, see, I got some of them new-fangled army rations. You just pull a tab and the stuff heats up all by itself. I swear. So we'll have some hot food and wrap you up in some blankets for a good sleep, and we can be ready for the worst the world can throw us tomorrow. What do you say?"

The boy nodded.

"Let's ride up a piece and see if we can't find a better place to camp. I'm not partial to porcupines creeping in my sleeping bag."

The boy giggled.
The hunter smiled and winked. He felt like giggling himself.

Daggert pushed on where the sun dipped below the horizon. But eventually, when it grew too dark to see, Stone refused to go another step. The big sorrel stomped his feet and shook his great head. He snorted when his ride pressed with his knees and gave the forward signal.

Daggert wanted to swear with frustration.

"What is it?" Leeza asked.

"We've got to stop," he muttered. He felt irrationally angry with her, as if it were her fault the sky had darkened, as if she had ordered Stone to halt. She'd brought more life into him than he'd felt in years. At the same time, if she weren't with him, he would continue, no matter the dangers.

"We can't stop!" she cried, once again proving that the lady had grit.

"We have to," he said. "It's too dangerous to keep going. Even knowing the terrain, I can't see three feet in front of me. We could ride right off a cliff or fall down a ravine or a sinkhole. I've got a flashlight, and it's a good one, but it won't do much if I'm on horseback. When the moon rises we might be able to ride another couple of hours. But in this light, we could go right past Enrique and never see him."

"And if you're right and Donny's killer is out there?"

For a moment her words took him to that carved tree on the top of Cima La Luz. He saw his son's maimed body. Saw it and felt it to his core. Daggert shook his head, as if throwing the image away. "Damn it, Leeza, there's not a thing I can do about the darkness. We can't keep going."

Not in the dark. Not with her to keep safe as well.

"If you're doing this for my benefit, you can forget about me," she barked, obviously unaware that he could no more forget about her than he could forget about food to eat or water to drink. "Enrique's all that's important."

"We're stopping," Daggert stated, and swung his leg over Stone, dismounting.

She didn't move. Her horse didn't, either, which meant the animal was too tired to traverse an inky-black terrain, and that it definitely was time to stop.

"What was that?" Leeza asked suddenly.

"What?" Daggert echoed. He cocked his head, listening. For half a second, he thought he heard Sancho.

"That!" Leeza cried.

Daggert registered the note of strained terror in her voice even as gooseflesh rippled across his body.

"Was that a whimper?"

Before Daggert could shush her so he could listen, she yelled, "Enrique? Enrique, it's okay!"

When the little boy didn't answer, but Daggert heard another whimper, he whispered for her to be quiet.

She immediately complied.

He whistled and felt his heart jolt when he heard Sancho whine, then bark.

"Sancho?" Leeza asked. "He's back?"

"Wait," Daggert said. "Something's holding him up. Otherwise he'd be here."

"Oh my God," she half sobbed. "What if—?"

Daggert pulled a flashlight from his saddlebags and cursed himself for not having brought two. He usually packed for every contingency, making it a rule to have two of everything in the event that something went amiss with one. But he'd never considered the need for two flashlights. After all, he was only one man. And if he was using the flashlight, he probably needed the other hand for his knife.

"Here, you take the flashlight and set up camp. I'll find Sancho."

"You take it. I'm fine," she said tersely. "I'll start a fire."

Daggert instinctively wanted to argue against lighting a fire, afraid Donny's killer would be able to easily spot them. But she was right. They needed the warmth and they needed to eat. And most of all, he needed the flashlight to find Sancho.

"Maybe Enrique has him," she said wistfully.

"Let's hope so," Daggert replied. But he didn't think the boy had anything to do with why Sancho hadn't come back to him all day. And he didn't believe Leeza thought so, either. He could see fear in her eyes.

He flicked on the flashlight and started away from her.

"Daggert?"

"Yes?" He turned.

"Be careful. Okay?"

Simple words, but they hit him like a fist to the gut. He strode back to her and pulled her to him for a hard, fierce kiss. But nothing in him felt fierce at that moment. He felt strangely unmanned, as if she'd torn his heart right out of him and held it in her hands. *"Denzhoné,"* he said gruffly, "I'll be right back."

Daggert was gone before she could even breathe again. "What does it mean?" she called out into the darkness, her eyes on the shaft of light bobbing off into the night.

"It means 'Beautiful Eyes'," he called back. *"Denzhoné Bidáá."*

The light moved deeper into the shadows and disappeared within seconds. She heard another whimper from Sancho and realized she was standing stock-still, her fingers scarcely holding the horse's reins.

Leeza secured the leather straps to a tree as she'd seen Daggert do several times now. She felt around on the ground for stones with which to build a campfire. She rummaged blindly through the saddlebags on Daggert's horse to find a lighter and the pot he used to boil water. She scratched herself on a sharp rock and stuck her hand into something cold and mushy before she'd gathered enough kindling to start a blaze.

Frantically wiping her hands on her pants, not even daring to think about what she'd encountered, she forced her fingers to stop shaking long enough to strike the lighter, and muttered her thanks as the flame illuminated her rough camp. She swiftly touched the fire to her small mound of kindling and couldn't restrain her smile of satisfaction when it caught and quickly flared into a small blaze.

Moving rapidly, gingerly snatching up dead twigs and branches from under the surrounding trees, she added them to the fire. Within minutes, she had a fairly good campfire going. The first thing she did was to check what she'd gotten into while fumbling around in the dark. It was a half-eaten tortilla smeared with peanut butter.

She stared at it for several seconds before turning back to the horses. "He's alive," she told them. "He's okay. And we'll find him."

Belle gave a low grunt as if agreeing with her.

Leeza pulled the collapsible water buckets from the saddlebags and filled them from the canteens Daggert had replenished at the river. After he'd replenished her.

She shivered, not because she was cold, but because the memory of his touch rushed through her with an almost painful sweep of unfamiliar emotions and longing.

Beautiful Eyes, he'd called her. But it wasn't the name, it was the way he'd said it that made her tremble with desire. He'd said it as if she possessed the most beautiful eyes in all the universe. As if he saw deep into her very soul and still found her lovely.

She wished that were true. Wished he could do that, and that what he might find would be as beautiful as the Apache word. But if she was honest—and if there was one thing Leeza Nelson prided herself on, it was being supposedly truthful—her soul wasn't spotless. She was as ruthless in her business ventures as Daggert was relentless in his search for Donny's killer. These were the thorns in their sides. Or maybe they were their Achilles' heels. The thought made the hair on the back of her neck prickle.

What would either of them be like without the thorns?

She almost screamed when Sancho suddenly materialized at the perimeter of the fire. He gave a low growl, then, upon recognizing her, uttered a bark of excitement and threw himself at her, his tail nearly dousing the flames. Knocking her from her feet, Sancho licked her face, jumped across her and whined happily.

"Get off her, you big oaf." Daggert was a disembodied voice and a beam of light coming out of the night.

"Where was he?" she asked, pushing Sancho away and struggling to her feet.

"Tied to a tree," Daggert said, stepping into the firelight.

Leeza could see his impotent fury. It was all he could do not to kick at something or throw himself onto Stone's back and ride out into the darkness. She sensed something more than his rage, as well—something dangerously close to fear. And the last thing she wanted to see on Daggert's face was anything remotely resembling fear.

She didn't suggest that Enrique might have tethered the dog, because what little boy, nine years old, would refuse the company of a great animal like Sancho? None. Even had he been afraid of the dog, he wouldn't have tied him to a tree. In that case, he wouldn't have approached the large setter at all.

No, she was sure that whoever had tied the dog to the tree was the same man who'd dropped the knife. And that the intricate design on the knife handle was the exact same carving that had appeared on the tree over young Donny's body.

"There are several people up here looking for Enrique," she reminded Daggert. "And you said you know them all."

He shot her a look loaded with meaning. "True. And one of them is Donny's killer."

"But he didn't hurt Sancho."

Sancho whined, sat down and held up his paw.

Leeza obliged him with a shake. The dog gave a sharp bark, followed by a low growling whine.

"What's the matter, boy?" she asked, remembering the dog having done the same thing the day before. And remembering Daggert frowning over it.

The tracker was frowning now, his eyes narrowed as he gazed at Sancho. "He's trying to tell us who it is. Like the way he collects things, he's using a gesture he does with someone to tell me who's out here on this mountain."

"But you don't know who?"

"Almost. I've seen it. I've seen Sancho doing this. But it's not coming to the surface who he does it with."

"Think," Leeza prompted. "Like you told me, you *know*."

"It's like when Donny disappeared and no one saw who took him. I think they all saw the man, only, it was just someone they all knew, someone they were so used to seeing that it didn't even register."

"Okay, we know one of the men is Jack, the former deputy marshal. Does he shake hands with Sancho when they run across each other?"

Daggert looked from Sancho to Leeza. He gave a sigh of frustration. "Maybe. I don't know. I just can't remember."

"And the grocers?"

A flash of recognition flickered across Daggert's face. "Always with Jenkins and sometimes with Greathouse, because they give him dog bisquits whenever they see him."

"How about the manager at Annie's café, Bill was it? Does he shake hands with Annie?"

Daggert ran his hand across his broad forehead. "I don't know. Maybe. I think so, but I'm not sure."

Leeza let it drop. There was no point in pushing Daggert; a person's memory was a mystery to even the most expert of psychiatrists, a layman like herself didn't have a clue how to probe it.

She said instead, "I found part of a peanut butter covered tortilla while you were gone."

He made a face.

She smiled. "I know, but at least it tells us Enrique's been this way exactly."

"It does at that," he said and looked away from her. He was hiding something from her. Something he'd discovered. She didn't know how she knew this, she just did.

"What?" she asked.

He turned his gaze back to hers.

"What aren't you telling me?" she asked. When he didn't answer, she pressed him. "I'd rather know the truth. No matter how bad it is."

"One of Enrique's gloves was tied to the end of the rope that held Sancho," he said.

Whatever she'd been expecting him to say, this wasn't it. She couldn't make sense of his words. They didn't frighten her; they were simply incomprehensible.

"The person who tied Sancho to that tree had Enrique's other glove. He wanted us to know that he has the boy. Or wants us to think so, anyway."

She drew in her breath with a hiss, then quickly said, "We can't know that."

"I can't think of another explanation."

"Maybe it's Jack, and he's letting us know he's found Enrique?"

Daggert didn't look away from her as he shook his head. "That doesn't make any sense, *Denzhoné*. If Jack found him, he'd shoot a few rounds in the air because he knows we're out searching. Unless he's not the person I always thought he was. No. This is someone playing with us."

Leeza wanted to protest, wanted to come up with another scenario, but couldn't. She realized that while she needed reassurance, Daggert wasn't the man to give it at the moment. He was caught up in his vengeful anger and needed comfort far more than she did. Every muscle in his body seemed to be stiff with the need to plunge into the darkness and find Enrique— and the man who might be holding him.

"The water's going to be hot enough soon," Leeza said, turning away from him.

She heard Daggert sigh behind her. "Good. Then maybe the moon will rise and we can get going again."

"Do you know what time it rises this time of month?" Leeza added another dry branch to the fire.

"Sometime around midnight," he said, rummaging in his saddlebags. He withdrew three pouches and dropped them into the boiling water. "This will have to serve us well. Our larder is almost empty."

"What?"

Daggert's eyes met hers briefly before he looked away. "I only packed for Sancho and me."

"And you fixed these for lunch, too, because you knew I hated the jerky," she said softly, remembering.

He gave a grunt that could have been assent. But she knew that's exactly what he'd done. The flare of attraction between them hadn't prompted that small and very important courtesy, simple human consideration had. Old-fashioned chivalry. He'd manufactured a reason to allow her to bathe and to eat a real meal.

A sharp stab of guilt assailed her. Had she not made such an issue of the jerky, he would have kept them moving toward Enrique. They wouldn't have stopped for so long. Wouldn't have made love on that grassy bank with the scent of pine as an aromatic aphrodisiac, and the gurgle of water as a symphonic backdrop.

They might have Enrique with them by now. They might have found Sancho hours sooner.

And she would never have known the sweet mystery of feeling totally in tune with another human being, that perfection of union she'd always heard about but had never once encountered.

She wanted to say some of this to Daggert, but saw by the tightness of his jaw that he was suffering a similar internal battle.

"It's my fault we lagged behind," she said firmly.

"The hell it is," he said roughly. He gave her a harsh glare.

She knew just how intense his anger could be, but she didn't back away from him. "We might have him by now."

Daggert's hand shot out and grabbed her arm, yanking her to him. "And if beggars had horses, they would ride."

"You know I'm telling the truth."

"What difference does it make?"

"It matters because you told me not to come with you. You told me I'd slow you down. And I did."

He gave her an odd look, one that mingled pain and a healthy dose of the bitterness he was named after. "But if you hadn't, I'd never have tasted you, *Denzhoné*. And God help me, that's all I've wanted to do from the first second I saw you."

Leeza knew that as tortured as he was by the need to keep going, as frustrated by the necessity of stopping and waiting for the sluggard moon to rise, he would be trapped between guilt and fury for as long as they were forced to wait. Pressed against him, held there by his firm grip, she gave a soft sigh.

"Then taste me. Please."

With a groan, he ground his lips against hers. She felt his fury, his fear for Enrique, his desire to be forging ahead and his longing for her. She gave herself to the kiss with a passion that seemed fueled directly from his.

She'd never felt so free with anyone before, nor so hungry.

His lips on her fanned a raging inferno inside her, making her almost desperate to feel him, to touch him intimately, to impress the memory of him on to her body. With abandon, she dug at his clothing, frantic to remove any obstacle between them. She was scarcely aware of him doing the same, so intent was she on reaching his smooth, muscled skin.

The warmth of him beneath her fingertips made her moan, and she lowered her mouth to the tiny buds of his nipples. She grazed them lightly with her teeth and relished his swift hiss and tightened grip.

He buried his hands in her hair and pulled her head back for a deep and thoroughly mind-shattering kiss, his tongue warring with hers, his lips plundering.

Her knees threatened to buckle and he released her only to push her blouse away and yank down her bra, so her breasts bounced free. His hands cupped them and lifted a nipple to his hot mouth. He suckled avidly, causing her to moan and a rush of molten heat to flood her loins. He transferred his attention to the other, leaving the first to be teased by the cold mountain air.

She fumbled with his belt buckle and yanked it free, pulling his jeans open with a swift tug on his zipper. She thrust her hands inside his briefs and captured the very essence of him in her grip. She ran her fingers down the full length of him, aroused by his heat, the throbbing need that pulsed within her grasp.

He unfastened her jeans with shaking hands and shoved them down a few inches as he pushed his fingers beneath the silk strip of her panties. He cupped her bottom and kneaded her rounded curves with powerful hunger, dragging her close, slowly rotating against her.

"Denzhoné," he growled. "You drive me insane."

And Leeza knew the insanity was contagious, for it slammed through her senses and robbed her of all rational thought. The entire world seemed made up of the two of them. Touching, aching, exploring, demanding. All barriers shed. His hands on her breasts. His fingers between her thighs. His mouth on her skin. His lips crushing hers. Her wrists bound with the long silk of his black hair. Her fingers tangling, pulling. Her mouth imploring him to take her now. Please, please now.

Lowering them to their heap of discarded clothing, Daggert rolled her on top of him and, even as she straddled him, lifted her and pulled her down over him. Sheathing him.

He cried out when she did, not in culmination, but in fierce triumph. His hands stroked her thighs, setting a rhythm as ancient as the stars themselves, and she rocked into him. Rising slightly, clenching him, she then lowered herself with aching slowness.

"Posting has its advantages," he said through gritted teeth, surprising a chuckle out of her and at the same time confusing her. It seemed so incredibly intimate, so very casually personal, as though they'd been lovers for years, had established inside jokes that underscored their private communication. Something she'd never done before because she'd never allowed anyone to get close enough to her to share laughter.

Daggert's hands found her breasts and he arched up to capture them with lips so thirsty she shook with the need to fill him.

But it was he who filled her. Driving deep, with sure steady strokes, taking her closer and closer to that precipice he'd introduced her to before.

Locked around him, feeling him within her body, rocking in his arms, Leeza realized that at this particular moment, this specific time, every single thing was right in the universe. Enrique would be found. Rancho Milagro would succeed. The world would spin around the sun and the sun around the galaxy. And this amazing man she was beginning to understand held her conflicted emotions in his hands every bit as firmly as he held her to him now.

With a primal cry, he drove up and into her, flinging her into that alternate place of rapture and sensation. Leeza knew he'd gone with her, lost on some blazing trail of culmination. She clung to his shoulders, arching away from him, encasing him, pulling him with her.

When he murmured his Apache name for her against her throat, she felt herself coming back, still shattered, but slowly finding the random bits of her mind. She gradually became aware of the chill of the night, the warmth of his body against hers, the heat of his lips at her collarbone.

She could hear the fire crackling, where moments before it had seemed a roar of conquest. And the stars no longer thundered her name.

She was once again just a confused woman in the arms of a haunted man.

But it seemed all right when he wrapped his arms closer around her and drew her beneath his chin, pacifying her with a slow, gentle swaying.

"Tell me about your childhood," she requested.

He sighed and continued his slow swaying, rocking motion. "I was raised on the reservation," he said. "It's not an easy life, but it's a good one. Children are prized in Apache culture and allowed much greater freedom than in the white world. I grew up in these mountains, spending most of my time up here."

"Sounds like heaven," she murmured, and was amazed to find herself believing that. Even a week ago she would have been aghast at the notion.

"Do you miss your ex-wife?" she asked, and blushed at the interpretation he might place on her question.

"We had grown apart long before Donny…went missing. She's remarried now and has a daughter. She's happy."

He hadn't answered her question, Leeza thought. But perhaps he had given her a more complete answer than she'd dreamed of.

"Will you promise me something?" she asked.

"I don't believe in promises," he answered. She could feel the words rumbling in his chest as if his heart was speaking directly to hers.

"Because they can be broken?"

"Because they are *always* broken."

"I keep them," she said. "I've never knowingly broken a promise."

His arms tightened. "As in everything, you're different there, as well. So, Leeza Nelson, will you promise me something?"

Leeza hesitated. She had the feeling that a tremendous weight hung in the balance of her answer. She could simply answer yes, and accept the responsibility of a promise she would walk through hell rather than break, or she could hedge, waiting to see what he was about to ask of her. It had always been her way to be cautious, to know what she was committing herself to before agreeing to sign on any dotted line.

Why was this any different?

It was. The man, the night, the mission they were engaged in, all these things conspired to make the notion of promises a wholly new concept.

"Yes," she said.

He stilled his slow swaying and raised his hands to her head, pulling her back a little so that her eyes met his. "I want you to promise me that when we find Enrique you won't stop me from going after the man who killed Donny."

"But—"

"No buts, *Denzhoné*. I want you to promise me now."

Leeza felt the importance of his words, the meaning behind them, and knew that at that exact moment, she would have promised him anything. *Anything.* Even if what he was asking her to do was to walk away from him, and that was the inherent subtext of his words.

"All right. Fine. I promise," she said, never letting

her eyes waver from his. "But you have to promise me something in return."

"No. No promises," he said.

"Then give me a pledge."

"Is there a difference?"

"Yes," she said. "A promise is freely given, a pledge requires security."

A chuckle rumbled through him, shaking them both. "You and your splitting meanings to a hair's width. All right, Leeza Nelson, what do you want as a pledge?"

She felt him move within her, a swift throb of withdrawal. She clenched around him as if denying that inevitability. "No," she said, not to his words, but to his breaking their connection. Then she stated, "Sancho."

"What?"

"I promised to let you go after you found Enrique, to let you go after Donny's killer. When you do…if you do…leave Sancho with me."

He was silent so long she was sure he was trying to figure out how to let her demand go unanswered. But finally, he sighed. "I don't know what you think that achieves, but okay. Sancho will stay with you."

"As a pledge."

"As a pledge."

"That's a vow."

"Splitting hairs again? You want a vow from me, *Denzhoné?* All right. I vow to find Enrique whole and sound and return him to you. And I vow to protect you while you are with me." He said the words with a solemnity due a prayer or a vow of such magnitude that nothing in heaven or on earth could ever revoke it. At the same time, she felt there was more he *wasn't* saying. "You say you don't break promises," he added. "I have never broken a vow."

Leeza wanted to remind him that he'd been married. Surely vows had been exchanged.

As was becoming usual with James Daggert, he seemed to read her mind. He gave the ghost of a chuckle, but there was no humor in it. "If you're thinking about my marriage, I can honestly tell you that, legally, Alma and I were never married. That's the Apache way. It's common. We promised to be faithful to each other as long as our time together lasted. There are no other commitments, except to family and children."

Leeza felt a stab of guilt for having so rapidly come up with a flaw in his logic. And she felt something she had no name for because she'd never felt it before. It made her ache and her eyes sting. It made her heart feel tight and her throat full. This nameless something hurt fiercely and felt glorious at one and the same time. Whatever the feeling was, it made her want to stay in the safety of his arms forever.

She had to ask him one more question, one that attached no promise or vow. "And if you find Donny's murderer? What then, James Daggert?"

He looked at her almost blankly, and she remembered him telling her there was nothing else in him but vengeance, nothing else but ridding the world of the monster who'd killed his son.

His eyes focused and his tawny eyes glittered in

the firelight. "I don't know, *Denzhoné*. I can't see beyond that time."

And sadly, Leeza knew he couldn't. But she didn't know who she felt more sorrow for, the vengeance-driven man holding her or the changing woman he held in his arms.

Chapter 9

The hunter wrapped the boy in a blanket from his pack. The boy scarcely stirred in his sleep. And why should he? His belly was full, he was safe in the company of a man he knew, and he would soon be reunited with his parents.

The kid hadn't talked much during their meal of army rations. But he had told the hunter about the aliens who took his parents away.

"And they're coming back to Cima La Luz," the boy had said. "For me."

"Didn't you like it at that Rancho Milagro place?"

A shutter had fallen over the boy's face. He'd shrugged. "It was okay," he'd mumbled.

"Were they mean to you?"

"No," the boy had said quickly.

"What about Leeza Nelson? Was she mean to you?"

The boy hunched a shoulder.

"She's out on this mountain somewhere," the hunter said.

The boy looked up at that. "Señora Leeza?"

"Sure enough."

The boy shook his head, contradicting him. "Not Señora Leeza. She doesn't like horses. She's afraid of them."

"I heard tell she's riding one after you."

"She doesn't even like me," the boy said.

"Maybe not, but she's coming after you, anyway."

The boy hadn't said anything for a long time, then had murmured, "She looks at me funny sometimes."

"Funny how, kid?"

"Like I remind her of someone. It makes her sad, I think."

"Everyone's saying it's her fault you ran away."

The boy had surprised him by shooting to his feet and glaring at him. "That's a lie!"

The hunter held up his hands. "Hey, don't take my head off, kid. I didn't say it."

"She's a real lady, Señora Leeza is. She showed me the stars."

"Constellations and such?"

The boy nodded, relaxing, then finally sat back down again.

"Why don't you show 'em to me?" the hunter asked. "Without a moon, they're pretty bright to-night."

The boy had pointed out the obvious ones and a couple the hunter was impressed a child would know.

The boy snored softly now, snug in his blanket, a little bug in a borrowed rug.

And the hunter pulled out his binoculars and zeroed in on the fire far below him on the mountainside. He couldn't make out any more than shadows around the fire's edge. But he knew Daggert and the woman were down there.

Daggert would be frustrated and angry, but made impotent to act by his very heroic nature. The tracker wouldn't leave her. And the woman would be worried sick about the little boy sleeping so peacefully at the hunter's side. Of course, he wouldn't be sleeping long. The moon was rising and it was time to move again.

What the boy had said about Leeza Nelson added a distinct flavor to the game at hand. There would be some crying before all was said and done.

His daddy used to tell him that.

He put his binoculars aside and pulled his toys from his saddlebag. He couldn't find his knife, the knife El Patron had presented him back in the good old days, the days of carving. He searched through his things, believing at first he'd just put the knife in a different pouch, then frantically rifling his packs. He'd had it that afternoon. It had to be here. When had he last seen it? When he'd tied up the dog? When he'd spotted signs of the boy?

His heart thundered. He felt as if he were unraveling, the way he felt sometimes when things were too busy at work, when too many people wanted too many *different things, when he had to wait on them with a smile instead of a knife.*

His knife!

But he still had his claws. The extensions of his soul.

Breathing heavily, desperate to subdue the fear rising in him, he lifted the boy's small jacket, discarded earlier at his suggestion. The boy wouldn't be needing it anymore, anyway.

The hunter wrapped his hands around the mountain lion's claws and savored the feel of the dry fur beneath his fingers. Relaxing somewhat, he slowly caressed the jacket with the tips of the claws, then dug deeper, and deeper still. He closed his eyes, feeling the power of the lion working through him.

When the jacket was in tatters, he moved to the boy's hat. He slashed the scrap of cloth and cardboard with a crosshatch pattern, destroying it with almost orgasmic intensity.

When he was finished, he carried them back down the mountainside and scattered them in the last meadow, where Daggert and Leeza Nelson were sure to find them.

There would be some crying before all was said and done.

The hunter grinned.

"Wake up, *Denzhoné*," Daggert murmured against Leeza's ear. "The moon's rising and we can make up for lost time."

Leeza snuggled against him for a second, her bare bottom curving into him. Instantly, his manhood rallied and he was suffused with a rush of renewed desire. He didn't think he would ever get enough of this woman. At least, not in her bed.

Her eyes popped open and she raised herself on an elbow. "We're going?"

"We should," he said, but he didn't want to. Only his fears for little Enrique would drag him from this bed now; his fears for the boy and his deep-seated need to find Donny's killer.

And even the latter reason wouldn't have been sufficient to propel him away from the warmth of her. He didn't want to think about the significance of that notion.

Watching her try to shake off her sleepiness, he felt a pang of guilt that he'd been tempted to sneak out of camp and search for Enrique on his own, leaving Sancho to watch over this lovely woman. But he hadn't left her, because he'd told her he would protect her while she was with him. And that wasn't a promise; it was a fact.

Before he'd whispered in her ear, urging her to wake, he'd watched this blond beauty sleeping at his side. Awake, she had the ability to look cold, disdaining, even imperious. In lovemaking, she seemed to slip into a wanton's skin, taking, giving and wallowing in the sheer glory of union. Asleep, she looked so vulnerable it made him hurt for her. Unlike most women, she had nothing of the child about her, but in sleep something fragile hovered about her parted lips, her lowered eyelids, her hand curved against her cheek.

If he didn't have the driving need, the fire in him

to find Donny's killer, the killer of all the missing ones, he thought he could very easily fall in love with this woman. She was so different as to be another breed of human altogether. She had passion, depth and an amazing simplicity. And she had a way of studying him that made him feel as if he were anomalous to anything she had ever seen.

With her lithe body, her icy-blue eyes, she reminded him of a palomino mare… He shook his head. No, that wasn't right. And then he had it. Once, years ago, he'd seen a picture of an arctic she-wolf poised on a snowbank, wary of the camera that snared her, but inherently unafraid of the possible danger. The wolf's ruff was raised and her tail half lowered, but she'd struck him as proud and unyielding, strong and willful. And so very alone, so very vulnerable.

When he'd seen the photo he'd wondered about the wolf, hoped that the photographer had just neglected to take a snapshot of her mate, because wolves mated for life and he hated to think of that lovely creature without a partner.

This was Leeza, an arctic wolf with a vulnerable heart.

He'd been unable to resist the lure of her silken hair, gilded almost silver in the rising moonlight. And she'd murmured, not in protest, but in a strangely content, susurrus purr, as surprising and alluring to him as the way she'd nestled against him when he'd taken her from her horse or caught her when she was so spent she couldn't get down by herself.

"Are you awake?" he asked.

"Yes. You can see in this light?"

''Yes,'' he replied and had to force himself to relax his hands, which he'd knotted into fists to stop himself from stroking her fine curves.

When he'd woken her, feeling her pressing against him, her incredible body so warm and inviting, so lush and beckoning, he found himself losing sight of everything but Leeza. Vengeance was the very last thing on his mind.

But he couldn't lose sight of finding Enrique.

They were dressed and out in the moonlight in less than fifteen minutes, having not unsaddled the horses or established a full camp.

Leeza's eyes finally adjusted to the dim light, and when she could see fairly clearly, she had the distinct feeling that the world was colored with a surrealist's paintbrush. The early autumn moon, waning now and low in the eastern sky, sent long black shadows from the trees and scrub, and splashed silver on the pine needles on the ground below. A screech-owl, etched in the moon's spilled gold, glided away like a wraith.

Once again she had the feeling of embarking on unfamiliar territory. It wasn't just that the surroundings were strange to her; her acceptance of the entire endeavor was as well. A risk taker by profession, she realized suddenly she had never been much of a gambler at heart.

She was as tidy in her life as Daggert was with his camp preparations. Everything had its place and every place was stamped with her personal seal of approval.

And tidy, well-organized Leeza Nelson had found passion and happiness in the wilds of a New Mexico mountain range with a tracker named James Daggert, while searching for a little boy who had run away because she hadn't even had the courage to offer the basic human kindness of drawing him into her arms.

The horses seemed eager to be moving up the mountain, and, as if disproving some of their riders' worry, stepped surely and carefully over stones and avoided any pitfalls.

Leeza was conscious of operating on several different levels. A part of her twisted with worry over Enrique. Another part focused on the difficult journey at hand. And still another remained in the conjoined sleeping bags, locked in Daggert's strong embrace.

Like an addict, she couldn't seem to get enough of the man. She craved him. She ached for him. And when he filled her, he filled her with a joy she'd never known before.

She pulled up on Belle's reins, the very thought of joy making her need to pause to assimilate this new notion.

"What?" Daggert asked. "Did you hear something?"

"No," she said. "Sorry. I'm fine." But she was lying to him. She was anything but fine. She was more confused than at any time in life since her parents had died. Was the last day she'd spent with them the last time she'd truly been conscious of having joy in her life? Probably not, because until it's gone, most children take such happiness for granted. But when had she begun to accept the lack of it in her life? And what a pathetic indictment—not the lack, for that was simply a fact, but the blind adherence to that absence of joy.

She urged Belle forward again, patting the horse's neck, assuring her that the brief halt had been nothing but silliness on her rider's part. But was it so silly a notion? When Leeza thought about the joy she felt in Daggert's arms, she'd literally had to stop to ponder the reality.

Joy.

Simple, exquisite joy.

She'd found a measure of happiness in her partners' company. They'd become heart sisters back in college, three orphans against the world. She'd envied her friend Jeannie's first family, the loving husband and the darling baby. She'd witnessed joy and peace on Jeannie's face. And the exquisite sorrow when a drunken driver had taken them out of this world, leaving her friend more than bereft—leaving her emotionally destitute. But Jeannie had found that joy for a second time at Rancho Milagro, with her federal marshal husband and her adopted children, and now, finally, a new child born of their love.

And Leeza's other friend and partner, Corrie, had found the path to her own identity and courage in coming to grips with her feelings about a teacher hero who cared more for other's lives than his own. And, as a result, she, too, had found that amazing state of grace, joy.

Leeza had always assumed that there was something inherently wrong with her, that the magic between a man and woman would be forever denied her, just as the heights of happiness were.

Corrie and Jeannie had found their loves by stepping completely outside of themselves in a new and wholly different terrain.

Wasn't Leeza doing something of the same thing? Hadn't she abandoned her lifelong career to come to Rancho Milagro? And hadn't she embarked on this journey to find Enrique with a woeful lack of knowledge and experience?

She'd told herself she owed Enrique her personal involvement in this search, but that wasn't all of it, was it? She'd come because she desperately wanted to find the boy, wanted to hold him in her arms and tell him she understood how much he hurt, how much she grieved with him, what a great kid he was, and how much she felt for him. And this was wholly new terrain for the emotionally distanced woman she'd always been.

She wanted to scream out that these had been the most traumatic days she'd ever spent in her life. And sigh that they'd also been the most wonderful.

Leeza thought about her friends back at the ranch and her financial empire in Washington, D.C. She'd left the world of venture capitalism to her well-trained assistants, but she'd continued to monitor every facet of her corporation, perhaps keeping the door open to return whenever she wanted. She'd assumed the financial reins at the ranch, exploring monetary opportunities every bit as assiduously as she'd ever investigated a possible business venture. But she hadn't changed. She'd been the same Leeza Nelson she'd always been, as well trained as her assistants, not by mentors, but rather by a strange, cold couple named John and Cora Nelson.

It took coming out onto a mountain in search of a little boy to make her see that she even could be someone other than the Leeza Nelson John and Cora had carefully engineered. That she was already changing.

This new Leeza, the one who found joy in Daggert's arms, could ride a horse without heart-pounding fear, could go for hours without a need to fill a seeming silence, could be a woman who would never let a lonely little boy go without a hug, without comfort.

This new Leeza could feel confident without having to be the only confident person. She could give as well as take. And at some point she'd have to thank the man who'd helped her discover her new self—thank him for seeing her first.

Chapter 10

Dawn sent fingers of cold rosy light across the tops of the pine trees, and Daggert frowned at the horizon. *Red sky at morning, sailors take warning.* A storm was coming. He'd felt it in the moist chill in the night. The very stillness now seemed to foretell approaching thunder.

Leeza had told him that first day that little Enrique was frightened of thunderstorms. Most children were at some point. Donny had been. *"Daddy? You won't let the lightning hurt me, right?"*

It had stormed the second night Donny was missing. Lightning had split the sky and released torrents of rain.

Daggert's mind skittered away from that thought and jumped ahead three days, to when he'd crested the peak of Cima La Luz.

Jack had tried to keep Daggert from seeing the sodden and battered body of his little boy. But he'd pushed past the deputy marshal.

He closed his eyes now, unwilling to see it again, wishing he'd complied with Jack's urgent plea.

"Are you okay?"

He opened his eyes. *Leeza.* Sharp tongued, warm bodied, as strong in her way as he was broken in his. "I'm fine," he said, and even to himself, he sounded curt. "We'll come up on a rise in a minute. You should be able to use your cell phone there." He pushed Stone to a brisker walk and soon reached the top of the hill.

A narrow meadow lined with yellowing aspen trees stretched before them, a passageway to the massive Cima La Luz looming above them in the northwest. Despite the thunderheads gathering, sunrise dappled the mountain clearing with a copper hue and lit the dew to a sparkling rose-gold.

But it wasn't the beauty of the meadow that stole Daggert's breath. It was the sight of a lump of clothing beneath a single scrub oak on the far side of the meadow.

Sancho had spied it, too, and was racing toward the tree, his body little more than a chocolate blur. Daggert whistled for him to stop. Sancho immediately dropped to the ground, a brown arrow pointing at tragedy.

"Hold up," he said, and he heard Leeza pull Belle to a stop. "Wait here."

He urged a restive Stone forward. The big horse shook his great head as if resisting the silent com-

mand, but picked his way across the clearing anyway.
Daggert told Sancho to stay back as he passed him,
dismounting a few feet away from the destroyed
clothing. Remnants of a child's jacket. Clawed by a
big cat. Destroyed. Flayed. And, dear God, the boy's
hat.

Sancho whined. Stone pawed the grass in the
meadow.

Everything in Daggert seemed to freeze. Once
again he was back on that mountain peak, Jack trying
to hold him back from the bloody lump beneath a tall
pine tree. *"Don't, man. You don't want to see this."*

But he had seen it. He'd burned it on the retinas
of his memory.

Every hope and dream he'd ever had lay beneath
that tree, ruined, destroyed, broken forever.

"There's no blood here," Leeza said quietly, un-
cannily honing in on his thoughts. When she placed
her hand on his shoulder and shook it slightly, he
realized she wasn't seeing the vision in his mind, she
was directing him to look more closely at the litter in
the meadow. "It's not real, see? Like the glove. Like
Sancho tied up. This is part of his game. Enrique's
not here."

Daggert was more grateful for this woman than
he'd ever been for anything on earth before. She was
a sweet voice of reason in a world seemingly gone
mad. It had gone sour four years before when Donny
didn't come home for dinner one night.

And now, with her soft voice—how had Daggert
ever imagined it could be icy, when it was rich with
untold depths?—and her warm hand on his shoulder,

her voice of reason in his ears, he could see the truth clearly spelled out in this wanton destruction marring the peaceful meadow.

Whatever methods the man had used before, his lunacy was laid bare now. No animal had done this. The sheer randomness of the claw marks indicated that insanity and not animal rage had created the tears. And whatever motives the madman had harbored before, Daggert was suddenly sure the monster was luring Leeza and himself higher up the mountain, to the very peak where he'd killed Donny.

When he could speak, Daggert said, "I want you to stay here." He felt unable to look around at her.

"No." Her refusal wasn't harsh; it was as soft as her skin and every bit as firm.

"He's playing with us. Leading us."

"Or waiting to separate us," she said with stark logic. "He's crazy. You said it yourself. And as such, we can't figure out his motives. For all we know, maybe he thinks he *is* a mountain lion."

Daggert looked at her finally and took in everything about her in a painful, jolting glance. She was utterly terrified, her lips pinched, her eyes too wide, her skin bleached with thoughts of what this madman might be doing to Enrique. Nevertheless, she wasn't giving in to her fears. She was actually demanding that he think it through logically.

"Denzhoné—"

"No. You're not going to sweet-talk me into this. You are not leaving me behind. You can arm me—I know you have a gun in one of those saddlebags. Or if it comes to that, I have the man's knife. We can plan a strategy, whatever you want. But I am not going to sit in this meadow waiting to hear a gunshot or a scream. Or wait to be killed myself. You promised me, Daggert.''

''I told you I don't believe in promises,'' he said harshly.

''You believe in vows. And you vowed not to leave me.''

That wasn't what he'd vowed, not quite. But he knew she'd won. And he knew he'd never admired anyone more than he did this woman, at this moment. ''Try your cell phone again. If you reach someone, tell them to send a helicopter to the meadow at the base of Cima La Luz. They won't be able to get any closer than that.''

Shaking outside, quaking within, Leeza flipped open the cell phone and swiftly pressed the speed dial button for Rancho Milagro. For a moment, she'd seriously thought that Daggert would forget about her, remember only his driving compulsion to avenge his son's death. She'd been sure that he would mount Stone, ride across the meadow and disappear into the woods beyond.

The shaft of pain she'd felt then was something unfathomable, too deep for mere words. She wasn't afraid of being left behind. She wasn't afraid of being alone in these mountains. She wasn't afraid of the killer Daggert believed was out there somewhere.

She wasn't even afraid of not finding Enrique—Daggert had vowed he would find the boy and she believed him with every fiber of her being.

She was starkly terrified of the prospect of not seeing Daggert again. Daggert the man, not the tracker.

The cell phone wasn't working. She tried it again, forcing herself to focus on the task literally in her hand, to let her mind erase the image of Daggert riding away from her.

She'd never considered a helicopter. If that very first morning she'd told Daggert about her suspicion that Enrique was going to Cima La Luz, would he have requested one then?

The point was moot because that time was past, and in the present, she couldn't get a signal.

"We'll try again later," he said. "If the storm lets you through." He swung his leg over his saddle.

No! Leeza wanted to cry out. But she didn't have to say anything; he waited until she remounted Belle.

"You okay?" he asked.

"Fine," she lied.

The hunter found the perfect place to secret the boy and wait for Daggert and Leeza Nelson.

The boy whined a little at the command to stay out of sight, but the hunter convinced him that he would never get to see his parents if he didn't hide now.

That he was telling the boy the absolute truth amused him.

Daggert felt the tension of the building storm. As they steadily made their way up the side of the mountain, zigzagging up the steep inclines, winding around boulders and pines, the pressure intensified. He noted jays screeching for their mates to return to their nests;

chickadees frantically foraging insects from the thick trunks of the pines; white-striped chipmunks racing into hollow deadfalls, their fat little mouths stuffed with pine nuts or whatever they'd managed to snatch from the ground before the downpour washed food away.

The sky seemed as angry and confused as Daggert felt inside. To the southeast, over the valley, azure patches mingled with puffy white streaks. To the northwest, ahead of them, dark purple thunderheads stampeded after their fluffier white cousins, building in their need to rage. A brownish tinge on the fringes of the storm foretold hail at lower elevations, where the temperature was warmer. In the mountains, it was anyone's guess what would happen—snow, hail, sleet and definitely rain. But the lightning flickering in the deepest purple indicated that rain was the least of their worries.

The Guadalupe Mountains sported more pockets of pure iron than almost any range in the entire mountainous state. And if pure iron was absent, the plentiful deposits of iron pyrite would lure the lightning as surely as any rod might.

The very top of the mountain was almost completely iron, iron pyrite and sheets of glass from the numerous times lightning had struck the sand there. Enrique had been right about the strange lights, but wrong about the source, Daggert thought. Cima La Luz was aptly named "Light Peak," but from the frequent bolts of lightning striking there and reflecting in the glassy surface, not from alien spaceships stealing hapless humans.

"Daggert?"

He half turned.

"I just wanted to tell you…"

He tensed, waiting, his heart beating, not knowing what this remarkable woman might say at this odd moment. He found himself hoping she'd reveal something that would change him forever. He shook his head, knowing that was impossible.

She fell silent.

"What?" he asked, the human part of him wanting her to continue to tell him, *Daggert, I wanted to tell you that I need you. Daggert, I wanted to tell you I've never felt like this before with anyone. Daggert, I want you. Forever.*

"Nothing. It doesn't matter," she said, and added, "Never mind."

Part of Daggert felt relieved. Whatever it was, he didn't need any distractions at this time. Just knowing she rode behind him was enough to drive him crazy. He had to think of the path ahead, the dangers around them, and keep his mind off the lovely woman on the horse that followed so readily.

At the same time, he was strangely disappointed. He had the feeling whatever she'd been about to say could be of such import that it might possibly alter the course of his life. His world. He remembered that at the start of their trek together, he'd had the odd sensation that, unlike all the others in his life, she wouldn't give up on him.

Stone snorted.

"You're right," Daggert murmured. "Wishful thinking."

"What?" Leeza asked. Too quickly?

Was she waiting for him to say something to her? Tell her something important? What could he tell her? She knew he wanted her; he'd have to be carved of bedrock not to. She knew he didn't believe in promises, and God only knew he had nothing to promise her. His future had died abruptly four years ago.

Still... Beauty, wit and cobalt-blue eyes. *Denzhoné Bidáá.*

"Nothing," he said, but he tasted the lie on his tongue and decided that lone word sounded ominously prophetic. There was nothing in his future. Nothing to offer anyone, let alone this woman. But perhaps, just perhaps, there was time to figure out what to say to this woman when the boy was found and Donny's killer made to atone.

And since when did Daggert think in terms of a future, any future, beyond finding the man who'd killed his son?

A vivid flash of light made a negative of the trees, turning them harsh white against a gray background. Less than a second later, a tremendous crack of thunder rocked the mountain and returned the sky to purple-black.

So much for the future, Daggert thought. The present had come crashing down.

Before he could even steady Stone enough to turn around, huge fat drops of icy rain pelted them.

Belle danced sideways at the explosion of light and the painful clap of thunder, almost unseating her rider. Instinctively, Leeza gripped the reins tighter and ran her hand down the horse's neck, as she'd seen Daggert do so often. The mare's muscles rippled nervously beneath her hand and she tossed her head, her ears laid back and her eyes white.

A freezing blast of rain pelted from the sky as if the lightning and thunder had ripped the very fabric of the universe.

Dimly, blinded by the rain, deafened by the thunder and desperate to keep Belle from bolting, Leeza caught Daggert's frantic hand signal to guide her horse closer to his. Below her, Sancho was crouching down, muzzle open, obviously barking at Belle, but Leeza couldn't hear the dog for the storm's cacophony.

Ducking her head to avoid the stinging rain, and already shivering despite her warm jacket, she forced down her fear as she gave Belle a gentle kick to get her moving forward again. *Enrique doesn't have a jacket,* she thought, and prayed he was out of the storm.

An icy wind whipped the pine branches and set them to waving furiously, each tree seeming to groan in protest at the insistent roar of storm. Lightning continued to flash, and thunder immediately followed.

Flanking Stone now, Belle seemed slightly easier, but Leeza knew how close the mare was to giving in to her atavistic terror. Almost as close as her rider was. She'd seldom been out in storms before—the world according to John and Cora Nelson precluded fools who didn't know how to get in out of the rain— and never one as violent as this.

Daggert reached out and clamped a hand around

her upper arm. He yelled something at her she couldn't make out over the raging storm. She tried meeting his eyes and it was like looking at him through a torrent of tears.

She was grateful she hadn't told him what was on her mind only moments before. She'd been about to blurt out her confused feelings—how she wanted him, the joy she felt in his company. The truth about not even knowing how she felt because she had no name for the emotions.

If she had, she'd be as vulnerable to him now as she was to this storm hammering them.

And as suddenly as the next flash of lightning, she realized that was exactly what she was: vulnerable to James Daggert. Open. Frightened. Wondering. Spellbound and more.

If he'd been able to see through the terrible rain, she knew he would have witnessed her every fledgling emotion dancing across her face, revealing her inner self, her heart, her very soul.

"Caves," he yelled at her.

She followed him, thinking there was some irony in their desperate search, this battle against the elements. Leeza Nelson had finally found a heart, and the man who'd showed her where it had been hidden was only concerned about getting in out of the rain.

The boy screamed when the huge thunderclap followed the bolt of lightning that had surely struck the top of Cima La Luz. The hunter growled at him to quiet down, it was only a storm, for chrissakes.

Even his superpowered binoculars couldn't make

*out a thing through the sheets of icy rain. But he knew
Daggert and Leeza Nelson were getting closer. All he
had to do was wait.*

*But fingering the mountain lion claws in his pock-
ets, he knew he didn't have much patience left. Didn't
they realize how difficult it was to be the smiling man
behind the counter instead of the animal that lived
within him?*

*At another clap of thunder, he let loose a scream
of pure blood lust.*

The boy behind him was utterly silent.

As caves went, Leeza thought it would never re-
semble Carlsbad Caverns—and made a mental note
to take Enrique there once they were back at the
ranch. But it was a pocket of shelter against the raging
storm.

Daggert hadn't dismounted, so neither did she, and
she was struck by the fact that the scallop in the bedrock was high enough to accommodate horses and
riders without any difficulty.

The rain slanted in the broad entrance, soaking the
horses' legs and drenching their riders' feet. But it
was relatively dry in the shallow upper interior. And
it stank of something dark and musty. Leeza hoped it
wasn't a bear's den or a mountain cat's lair.

She shuddered, thinking about Enrique, pleading
with the powers that governed the universe that he
wasn't out in this storm, but taking shelter in a cave
similar to this one.

''Are you okay?'' Daggert asked, his voice rough
with tension.

''How long will this last?'' she inquired by way of an answer.

He shrugged. Huge droplets of water spilled from his long hair like diamonds from a jeweler's tumbler. She recalled how that silky mantle had covered her, how it had snared her fingers, how it had felt teasing her skin.

Sancho sat and whined piteously. He raised a paw and barked at Daggert.

Leeza saw the flash of recognition cross Daggert's face. ''Bill Thompkins,'' he said.

''Who?''

''Bill from Annie's Café.'' He said it with a note of wonder in his voice.

Leeza understood. He'd made the connection of Sancho's gesture with the half-forgotten memory in his head. ''Because he shakes hands with Sancho?'' she asked.

''Because Sancho always whines when Bill touches him.''

Ever since Daggert had demanded to know who Jeannie had said was up on the mountain looking for Enrique, Leeza had been straining to remember the three names her friend had mentioned on the cell phone. Leeza had been unable to conjure up a face for either Jenkins or Greathouse, the grocers, but she had a perfect image of Jack, Chance's former deputy marshal.

But once she'd gotten past the unfamiliar name, perhaps never really having heard it, she'd remembered Bill Thompkins perfectly. Her heart sank now, thinking about the manager of Annie's Café. She hadn't particularly cared for him, for the way he didn't quite meet her eyes whenever the Milagro gang had gone there, or the way his gaze seemed to undress her. She'd commented on it to Corrie one time: "He makes me think of a man who does dirty things in his basement."

She hadn't known the half of it. But Sancho had. "He knew," she breathed. "What was hidden behind the man's face."

As if agreeing with her, Sancho barked, turned to face the rain and barked again with greater urgency.

A strangely garbled animal scream cut through the storm's roar. Because of the curvature of the cave, the sound could have come from anywhere—deeper in the mountains, higher above them or from behind the very walls of the cave itself.

"Dear God," she said, automatically cringing. "What animal made that sound?"

Sancho ran out into the rain, barking furiously, his head lowered, his neck ruff raised.

"That was no animal," Daggert growled.

Leeza put her hand on his arm. Even through the thickness of his sheepskin jacket, she could feel the tensile strength of his rigid muscles.

"*Denzhoné*, I want you to stay here. I mean it. I've got to go. That's him. He has the boy. I know it."

Leeza saw that Daggert's knuckles were white with the fierceness of his grip on Stone's reins. A muscle worked in his jaw.

"Go then," she said.

With an odd look at her that seemed filled with unspoken need, he was gone.

"But you're crazy if you think you're going alone," she added, blindly following him into the storm.

As if responding to his scream, the storm abated just enough to allow the hunter to hear the frantic barking of Daggert's dog, Sancho.

When he was Bill Thompkins, he would shake hands with the setter. It always amused him that the dog could see the animal in him, and that his master, the great and powerful tracker, couldn't. It was a game he would play—teasing the dog into fear. Any dog was afraid of a mountain lion. Smart dog. Good dog.

He pulled his hunting rifle from his saddle and aimed it down the mountain, ignoring the rain, sighting the scope on the only trail Daggert could possibly take.

He wouldn't kill him. No. He wanted Daggert to see exactly what his little boy had gone through, because he'd had to pay for his daddy's crossing boundaries, invading the hunter's territory. He wanted Daggert to be powerless to stop him from reenacting his son's death scene, with Enrique Dominguez and Leeza Nelson in the leading roles.

A two-fer. The hunter giggled.

Then Daggert would see the face of his ancestors. The hunter wrapped his finger around the trigger.

Chapter 11

Daggert felt as if his heart was being ripped in two. Half of it remained in the cave with Leeza, the other half surged ahead, seeking the madman who had another little boy in his grasp.

Ruthlessly, Daggert focused his attention on trying to plot ways to extricate the child from the monster's clutches. But the truth was, he had no idea what he was facing.

The only thing he had in his favor was a good horse, a smart dog and a burning need to save the boy.

Squinting through the rain, his eyes on Sancho, Daggert realized he had yet another advantage, one that couldn't have occurred to him in the past four years. The last three days had given him something to live for.

He pulled his knife from inside his sheepskin coat. He had a Smith and Wesson in the holster on his saddle, but, as always, he preferred the deadly accuracy of his knife.

The storm had lessened but was by no means finished raging yet. And judging from the madman's scream, more than a storm waited for him on the mountaintop.

Daggert lowered his head against the rain and sought the fury that had sustained him so thoroughly for the past four years. Like the storm, his rage wasn't finished, but he knew something was different now. He felt it had splintered, worry about Leeza and Enrique overshadowing his hatred of the fiend who'd killed Donny. But his worry also fanned a whole new set of emotions.

He pulled up on Stone's reins, instinct warning him that charging up the mountain could be a deadly mistake for the boy's sake. But he was also held back by emotions that took in the possibility of futures, hopes and dreams. Emotions that embraced the possibility of escorting Leeza Nelson to a movie or out to dinner. Something simple, something normal…and something so alien to him.

He was struck by the awareness that he didn't know what kind of food she liked, what kind of movies she watched, what kind of music she listened to. He'd spent three intense days with the most remarkable woman in the world and he didn't even know what would make her laugh or why she might cry. He didn't even really understand what she did for a living beyond making bundles of money.

As he hesitated before rounding the last sharp curve on the trail leading to the upper caves and the very top of Cima La Luz, he felt the weight of being the instrument of justice against this man who had stolen so much from him.

And from others.

Cold rain pelted Daggert's face and soaked his jeans. And seeped into his soul. What was wrong was obvious: a madman had little Enrique Dominguez in his control. How to set it right wasn't so clear.

Daggert had spent the last four years preparing for, concentrating on this single moment, and now that it was literally at hand, he struggled with feelings of sharp ambivalence.

Hesitating at the last curve of this mountain trail, not afraid of the confrontation sure to come, but no longer certain of his need to vanquish Donny's killer, he realized this was the first moment he'd considered that there were others like him out there—grieving family, survivors lost to anything but vengeance or justice. Others who desperately needed some measure of closure. The husband of the housewife who had gone out for an afternoon stroll on the outskirts of town and been found miles away, ripped to pieces the same way Donny had been. The hiker who'd seemingly fell, but lay spread-eagled beneath a cliff, the rim of which held a set of footprints that didn't match his hiking boots. The young couple necking in the wrong place, both mauled beyond recognition, and the trembling aunt who had been forced to provide toothbrushes to confirm their identities, as DNA was the only recognizable identifier for them.

Every one of those people harbored some of the rage he did. And every one of them deserved resolution. Justice. Vengeance.

Sancho barked frantically and stopped at the turn in the trail.

Daggert knew the moment for which he'd been waiting for four long years was finally at hand.

Instead of feeling fury rise in him, the need for an end to the four-year nightmare thrumming through his veins, he discovered a strange effervescence, a buoyant lightness.

He felt free. Stripped clean. As if he might be allowed to start anew.

And if he was lucky, very very lucky, that new start might just include Leeza Nelson.

She'd asked him what he would do when he caught up with Donny's killer.

He'd told her he would kill the man, and beyond that moment, he didn't know. He'd told her the truth, as he saw it then. Just yesterday.

Now he had an answer for her. He would finally murder the rage that had held him in its thrall for the past four years.

He would kill the fury roiling in him, throw sand on the fiery rage that burned everyone around him. He would be able to sleep again, appreciate the good mountain air.

And possibly, just possibly, he would be able to give his heart again.

Sancho barked and raced back to him, as if needing to speed his master along. The setter scrabbled on the wet trail, then whirled around and leaped up the mountain again. He careened from rock to rock, more antelope than dog now, a brown force of nature with Bill Thompkins's scream leading him directly to the crazy bastard. And bringing Thompkins's nemesis right behind him, riding on the broad back of an incredible horse named Stone.

Daggert urged Stone forward and upward, and the mighty animal with the huge heart lunged toward the sharply angled curve and within seconds brought them around to face the cave-pocked cliffs leading to the very top of the cloud-obscured Cima La Luz.

Lightning flickered in the blackened sky above the peak, and ghostly clouds, white wisps of moisture, snaked down over the ledges.

Sancho, looking up at the cliffs, barked furiously, shaking with the intensity of his desperate need to alert Daggert to danger.

Daggert leaned forward in his saddle and heard the crack of thunder at precisely the same moment Stone suddenly shrieked and reared. Stunned by his mount's uncharacteristic reaction, Daggert jerked back, pulling on the reins, shouting for the horse to calm down.

He felt something sharp and hot rip into his shoulder. He understood that Stone had been wiser than he and had been trying to avoid the danger that had just struck his rider.

Whatever hit him yanked Daggert from Stone's back with a hammer-drill force that slammed him to the sodden ground. Pressed against the wet pine needles, he realized with almost perfect clarity that the crack he'd heard hadn't been thunder, but the sharp report of a high-powered rifle.

The impact had knocked the wind from his lungs, and he tasted the coppery tang of blood on his lips. He must have cut his mouth during the fall, he realized with an almost idle curiosity.

He couldn't seem to breathe and he wondered if he'd been hit worse than he thought. He half expected his life to flash before his eyes, as he'd always heard it did at the precise moment of death, but instead he saw Leeza's blue, terrified eyes staring down at him from her pale, shocked features.

She hadn't listened to him. Hadn't stayed behind in the cave, safely waiting for him. Why had he even thought she would? It wasn't her way to stay behind. Not in anything.

He mouthed her name.

He was conscious of breaking his vow to her and knew she'd take care of Sancho and Stone.

He should have let her see some of what was in his heart.

He should have given her that much.

When Leeza heard the thunder and saw Daggert fall from a rearing Stone, her heart jolted so painfully she couldn't breathe.

Belle sidled to the left and shook her head in swift denial. When Leeza tried pressing her forward, every pore in her body wanting to be with the man lying so still on the wet embankment, her horse seemed to catch her fear and did a prancing dance of terror.

Sancho barked and Belle shuddered as a riderless Stone raced past them, tearing down the mountain as if his hooves had been set on.

''God, no,'' Leeza choked out, then cried, ''Daggert!''

Inexperienced at tracking as she was, she wasn't stupid. She knew Stone hadn't shied from a fear of lightning and that Daggert hadn't fallen to the ground because his horse had spooked.

That last deafening crack of sound that ripped the sky wasn't thunder; James Daggert had been shot.

In a strange time distortion, the whole universe became elastic and pliable. When she met Daggert's pain-filled gaze and, with a shock, believed that he wasn't thinking of the madman atop the mountain, but was thinking of *her,* the moment seemed to last a lifetime.

She clearly saw an alternate future in his eyes, a future with laughter, children, lazy days beneath a cerulean sky.

And she saw the cold rain beating down on the man who had discovered her heart and given it to her.

And then his eyes seemed to glaze over, and with a sob of the deepest agony, she realized he could no longer see her.

He lay perfectly still on a bed of wet pine needles and mud. One of his hands was outstretched as if reaching for her.

The hunter was scared.

Daggert wasn't supposed to die yet. He had to suffer. That was how the game was supposed to be played. Daggert was breaking the rules again.

He heard a noise behind him and turned in time to

see the flash of white—Enrique's tennis shoes disappearing up a crack in the cave.

He let loose another animal cry, this one of undiluted rage. He lunged for the boy, but only scrabbled against the cave's roof; the boy was already gone, having climbed to the ledge above the cave.

No! he screamed, the man in him coming to the surface amidst his fear and fury.

Leeza had the fleeting thought that she'd been better off not knowing that she had a heart; understanding it existed only let more pain penetrate the deepest recesses of it.

"No-no-no," she murmured, but inside she felt a scream of pure anguish rising and threatening to break free, a scream every bit as animalistic as the madman's on the mountain above her.

She felt as if she would choke on the taste of the pain.

As if he were attuned to her, she heard another of the monster's shrieks.

Instantly her skin crawled and, out of the anguish inside her, a burning pillar of rage exploded into reality.

She'd been uncomfortable in the house of John and Cora Nelson; she'd fought her way to the very pinnacle of venture capitalism; she'd despaired over Enrique's running away…but she'd never embraced the fury against fate. She felt it now and understood Daggert, really understood him for the first time. She had wondered what motivated the man, how he could continue as a tracker when he'd lost his own son.

She knew the answer now: a blazing inferno of utter rage had fueled him, had allowed him to keep going. As it was sustaining her.

She set her jaw and leaned forward on Belle. Daggert's feelings were hers now. She felt them flooding her veins, infusing her with a dark strength and hot determination. And a black, dark rage filled the heart she'd only so recently discovered she possessed.

The time distortion shattered and abruptly, she could feel the cold rain, was aware of the lightning overhead, the pull of the earth. Only seconds had passed. A blink in the cosmic eye.

As if understanding the situation, Sancho had half turned back to Daggert. But the madman's next scream stopped him in his tracks. The dog whipped back around and with a ferocious growl, launched himself toward the cliffs leading to the very peak of this horrible mountain. A moment later he again stopped sharply.

Leeza, following on Belle, one with her horse, one with the fury inside her, dragged on the reins, and the mare slithered on the muddy track. Automatically, Leeza turned to see what Sancho was focused on. A wave of adrenaline swept through her, almost making her ill.

High on a clifftop, Enrique was picking his way along a narrow ledge, his tiny body pummeled by freezing rain and his thin cotton shirt buffeted by strong winds.

She heard the madman yell *"No!"* and knew that by some miracle Enrique had managed to escape him. Probably while the man was shooting Daggert.

Terror for Enrique kept the fury in her soul honed to a razor's sharpness, and she ruthlessly kicked Belle on up the dangerous path. As she rocked with the horse's powerful stride up the slippery trail, she frantically dug in her front pack, not for her cell phone, the small device she'd often used as a weapon in her business, but for the killer's beautiful and evil knife, her fury's weapon of choice on this bleak day.

She had it in her hands, and without conscious thought depressed the button that sprang the serrated blade free from its hiding place inside the intricate hilt.

She didn't look back, didn't dare, for she knew if she did she would see her heart lying on the ground with the man who had taught her she owned one.

Chapter 12

"Jesus. It's James Daggert," a voice Daggert dimly recognized said. "I thought that was his horse running toward that meadow."

"Is he dead?"

"He's not," Daggert answered. He felt as if he were talking around a sackful of marbles. For a split second, disoriented and confused, he couldn't think why he was lying facedown in pine needles and mud.

Then memory slammed into him. *"Leeza!"* he growled. He turned his head, ignoring the sharp pain in his shoulder, and saw a grizzled Jack Dawson, former U.S. deputy marshal, bending over him, worry carving lines of stress on an already well wrinkled face.

"Where is she?" Jack asked.

"She went to the top," Daggert said. "Get me up."

Jack extended a hand. The other man, John Jenkins—owner of Jenkins's IGA and Farmer's Market—slid down the embankment and shoved a hand beneath Daggert's arm.

With their combined help, Daggert struggled to his feet. He swayed a bit but his head was clearing.

"Somebody shot you?" Jack asked.

Daggert looked at him stupidly for a full two seconds, then followed Jack's gaze to the hole in his jacket, the stain of red shining darkly on the dampened cloth.

"The same man who killed my son," he said.

Jack Dawson looked from the hole in Daggert's shoulder to the ground and finally met Daggert's eyes.

Daggert realized the man had no way of knowing that a madman had little Enrique, could even have Leeza by now.

"Bill Thompkins," he said tersely.

"Thompkins? From Annie's Café?" Jenkins asked. "He *shot* you? Why?"

Daggert never looked away from Jack Dawson's eyes. The man might be retired, and may not have listened when he was still a deputy marshal, but the lawman in him was listening now. "He's Donny's murderer."

Jack's gaze didn't flinch, though a dull flush stained his cheeks. "And he's got the Milagro kid?"

Daggert nodded.

"What are you talking about?" Jenkins asked. "Thompkins is in Rotary with me."

Daggert ignored him.

"How long has Leeza been up there?" Jack asked.

Daggert was searching the ground for his knife. "A few minutes. Not more than five." He found it and dried the blade on his shirt.

"Let me bind that shoulder," Jack said.

"Forget it," Daggert said. "We have to move fast."

From somewhere above them, Leeza screamed.

Leeza dragged on Belle's reins and the mare skidded to a stop, snorting and pawing the ground. Some thirty feet above them, Enrique inched along a narrow ledge, the storm trying to pry him from his already precarious safety. She wanted to call out in encouragement, but was afraid she would startle him into falling.

But seconds later, Bill Thompkins burst from an opening in the cliff face almost directly beneath the boy. He was yelling obscenities at him and leaping up, trying to grab the boy's feet.

Leeza screamed a warning.

Instead of falling, Enrique shouted her name. *"Leeza! Ayudame!"* he yelled, even as he kicked out at the man clambering after him.

Bill Thompkins whirled around and let loose a primitive growl of rage. His eyes were something out of a nightmare, the whites showing fully around the dark, crazed irises. She hadn't been impressed with the man's looks when she'd seen him in Annie's Café, but there he'd been in some semblance of control. Now his face was contorted with rage, his lips

moist with his own spittle, his teeth bared and snap-
ping. He flailed what looked like a glove at her, and
she realized it was a mountain lion's paw, claws fully
extended and glittering in the rain.

Even as she wanted to gag in horror, Sancho
launched himself toward the cliffs. Instinct drove
Leeza, and she bent over Belle's neck and forced the
mare to a full gallop. From a standstill to a dead run,
the horse seemed to fly across the broad clearing leading to the cave pockets.

Lightning flashed overhead and thunder rolled
across the mountaintop. Leeza felt she was soaring on
anger and fear, trusting the horse to wing her to Enrique's rescue, never taking her eyes from the tableau
on the cliffs above her.

"Leave him alone!" she yelled at Bill Thompkins.

"You're not playing the game right," Thompkins
screamed back as he lunged at Enrique.

Belle came to a shuddering stop mere inches from
the base of the limestone-and-iron wall. Leeza let the
forward propulsion catapult her from her saddle. She
caught at a protruding rock and scrambled toward the
lowest cave.

Sancho had already discovered a way up the dangerous ledges and was actually wagging his tail as he
leaped from one narrow outcropping to the next.

Enrique wriggled away from the madman, though
to Leeza it seemed the man's insanity would lend him
the power to claw his way up the rock face, as an
animal might do.

"Hey, Thompkins," she called out.

His head swiveled in her direction and a flash of

human recognition flickered in his eyes, only to be replaced by a fury so intense that Leeza involuntarily shrank back against the rock wall she clung to.

He snarled at her and waved that battered and shedding claw.

"You want to go after someone, try someone a little closer to your size," she yelled at him. Her voice was high-pitched with fear, but the words sliced through the storm's roar. She held out his own knife and waggled it at him. And she knew she could use it.

A scream of pure rage came from him at the sight of his artifact in her hand. He didn't shift around as she'd anticipated, but pushed away from the cliff and all too nimbly leaped down to the narrow ledge she balanced upon.

He swung his hand down in a slicing motion, and Leeza cried out as the vicious claws tore through her jacket.

Daggert felt as though he was running through quicksand trying to reach Leeza and Enrique.

When she'd galloped straight toward the cliff, his heart had literally been in his throat.

"Who the hell does she think she is? Annie Oakley?" Jack panted from behind him.

Jenkins, lagging some ten feet behind Jack, let loose a girlish shriek.

But Daggert didn't pause in his loping run. His eyes darted from the woman he needed, to the boy he had to save for her. If he could get between Leeza and Thompkins, he might be able to deflect the man's attention long enough to allow her to get to the boy.

Then Thompkins seemed to perform magic, leaping from one of the cliff ledges to land on the outcropping below.

Daggert gave a cry of primal rage as Thompkins slashed at Leeza's shoulder with his deadly trophy of another of his kills. *"Leeza!"*

For a moment, Leeza believed she'd conjured Daggert's voice out of the storm, her mind creating an auditory hallucination to help her survive this terrifying encounter with a man so crazed as to seem preternatural, a beast created from all nightmares combined.

"Leeza!" Daggert's voice called again.

With a shock wave of joy so intense that it seemed to steal every vestige of strength from her, she sank against the slick walls, realizing that Daggert wasn't dead, after all. Not lost to her. Not gone forever.

Hot tears flooded her vision and her strength returned. She pushed away from the wall, holding out the murderer's knife, fully prepared to fight the man-creature with it.

"Get Enrique," she commanded Daggert, not daring to look away from the madman in front of her.

"Jump, *Denzhoné!* Jump down now!"

Thompkins growled and swiped at her with those claws. To her horror, she now saw that he held a paw in each hand, and he hunched down, his low growling audible over the wind and rain.

She waved his knife at him, taunting him, daring

him, afraid of him, but more fearful of what he would do if she showed any sign of fear.

Daggert signaled for Jack to go after Enrique, and whistled at Sancho to have him stop the boy before he could clear the top of the cliff face. It was as equally dangerous up on the iron-and-glass peak of the Cima as it was on the ledges with a crazy man after him. Lightning wasn't fussy about who it struck.

When the man lunged at Leeza, lion's paws outstretched and strangely terrifying, Daggert's heart seemed to freeze.

"Oh my God," Jenkins said from behind him. "That really is Bill Thompkins. What does he think he's doing?"

Daggert jumped for the lowest cave and missed, the wound in his shoulder throwing him off balance.

Surprising him, Jenkins rushed forward and threw himself down on his hands and knees. "Here," he yelled. "Use me."

The couple of extra feet of a boost Jenkins's back offered did the trick, and Daggert swung up and onto the ledge behind Leeza and Thompkins. And heard his knife clatter to the sodden bedrock below.

Jenkins yelped.

Thompkins had Leeza pressed against the rock wall and was flailing at her with those deadly paws. Even over the storm and the man's insane growling, Daggert could hear material being rent and slashed.

He grabbed Thompkins by the back of his coat collar and jerked him around, then felt the claws tear through his shirt, scratching him. With a cry of rage, he drove his fist into the madman's face.

Daggert shook his head, trying to rid himself of the image of this man pressed against Leeza, of the cuts she'd surely sustained. He hit the man again.

For a split second the animal in Thompkins disappeared, to be replaced by a human look of fear and pain. His head snapped back and his lower lip burst in a splash of red.

But when he lifted his head almost immediately, the animal had returned, and the snarling teeth, bloodied and red, were somehow more frightening in their garish color.

Before Thompkins could fully recover, Daggert plowed his fist into the man's midsection, even as the deadly claws swiped at his face. He felt the razor sharp claws meet his cold skin and felt the immediate sting of contact. An upper cut to Thompkins's jaw sent the man tumbling back and slamming against the wet wall behind him. But he wasn't spent. As crazy people often did, he seemed to find a strength that defied simple laws of physics. He pushed away from the wall, and didn't lunge for Daggert, but for Leeza.

She gave a short scream and raised the knife in a swift, defensive thrust as he rammed into her.

A look of almost comedic surprise crossed Thompkins's face.

He pushed back from her, his eyes scrunched nearly shut, his bloodied mouth blubbery. "But you're the one who's supposed to be hurt," he said clearly. "You need to learn a lesson."

Leeza shuddered and shoved at him, pushing him directly into Daggert's hands.

Almost dully, Daggert took in the serrated knife sticking out of the man's thigh. *That has to hurt,* he thought with surprising humor. Only three days in Leeza Nelson's company, and her wit had snaked into his head.

"Good job," he told her. It was hardly a deadly wound, but certainly effective in that it had taken the fight out of him.

Daggert spun Thompkins around in a ungraceful parody of a two-step twirl, and the man sank to the ledge with a keening wail, one leg dangling over the edge, the other tucked beneath him. "She hurt me," he cried. "She *hurt* me."

Feeling sick, wondering about the vagaries of fate that had taken his knife from him just when he most needed it in the world, Daggert massaged his hand, keeping a wary eye on the madman at his feet.

Hugging a sliced hand to her side, Leeza watched as Daggert lifted one of his boots. She knew he could easily kick the man from the ledge and let gravity finish him off. And not a soul on earth would blame him for it.

She thought of her own deeds that day, the dark rage she'd felt when she saw Daggert lying on the ground, the fury that had given her the strength and courage to fight the crazed Bill Thompkins. She would have killed the man herself rather than let him get to Enrique. Should have killed him for what he'd done to Daggert's son, Daggert himself.

She had promised Daggert to let him go for Thompkins once Enrique was safe.

She craned her neck and saw Jack Dawson on a ledge high above them, trying to coax the boy down to him. Sancho was barking at the boy from another point slightly up and to the child's right. The boy wasn't paying them any attention. His whole focus was on her, his eyes strained and his little face drawn with terror.

She raised her hand at him and offered him a tremulous smile.

He burst into tears. She felt like doing the same.

Enrique was safe. He would be okay.

She closed her eyes, knowing this was Daggert's moment. She willed him not to kill Thompkins, but she wouldn't stop him.

After an internal struggle that left him shaking, he slowly lowered his boot back to the ledge. He stood staring down at the broken man beneath him.

"Why?" he asked.

Thompkins didn't look up, continuing to sit on the ledge, rocking in the diminishing rain, tears of pain smearing the blood on his lips.

"Why did you kill my son?" Daggert elaborated.

Thompkins shrank away from the quiet menace in Daggert's voice. "I had to," he whined. "You had to be stopped. You were crossing my boundaries. You weren't supposed to keep tracking me, but you did anyway."

Leeza felt Daggert's painful intake of air as if the crazy man's words had pummeled her own body.

"You sick bastard," Daggert said, and added something in Apache.

Thompkins flinched.

"How many?"

Jack shouted down, "Bill Thompkins, you are under arrest. You have the right to remain silent, for anything you say can, and will, be used against you in a court of law. You have the right to consult with an attorney. If you cannot afford one, the court will appoint one for you at no charge. Don't do anything, Daggert. Let the law take it from here."

Below them, Jenkins ran into view, staring wildly up at the trio on the narrow ledge. "Are you okay up there?" he called.

Thompkins leaned forward. "John. Are you here to get me?"

A spasm of something akin to revulsion crossed Jenkins's features, but after a quick look at Dawson and Daggert, he nodded. "Sure am, buddy. Can you get down here?"

"I don't think so. I'm bleeding. See? She stuck my knife in my leg."

"How many others did you kill?" Daggert asked. His question was so filled with tension that it seemed to dry up the storm which, as quickly as it had burst upon them, suddenly abated.

To Leeza it felt that even the heavens waited for the man's answer to Daggert's question.

Thompkins hunched away, but turned a face so filled with hatred in Daggert's direction that Leeza felt herself go numb. "More than you'll ever find, half-breed, even if you track for a hundred years."

Daggert almost gently pushed him from the cliff.

"Oh my God!" Jenkins yelled.

Thompkins screamed and swore when he slammed into the ground. "You hurt me!" he yelled up at Daggert.

Leeza leaned against the wet rock face and closed her eyes. She fought the smile that threatened to come to the surface.

"*Denzhoné,*" Daggert said, and his callused hand caressed her cheek and slid into her wet hair.

Chapter 13

Jack Dawson used his cell phone—which miraculously worked—to call for a helicopter. He spoke directly with Chance Salazar, his former boss, and was promised a chopper would be in the meadow below the Cima in less than an hour.

Leeza listened to his conversation with Chance as though a wall of glass separated them. How to get them home was the furthest thing from her mind; she was busy wrapping a blanket around Enrique.

Typical of New Mexico storms, the one that had created such havoc less than thirty minutes earlier had blown itself out, and already the sun was beating down, drying the grasses, heating the rock wall she sat on.

"I was pretty scared," Enrique said, and although his eyes were still too large in his face, he didn't look very frightened anymore. He was flushed with the aftermath of such a big adventure.

She used a dry washcloth to blot the last of the moisture from his hair.

"My knees are still knocking," she admitted with a smile.

The boy's smile faltered as he looked up at her. "Are you mad at me?"

She thought of him calling out her name and begging her in Spanish to help him. Still, she almost responded with the John and Cora Nelson litany of "What you did was wrong. I'm sure you see that—" Even as the words rose to her lips, she swallowed them. Except for Daggert, nothing else had ever tasted so right. "I was scared for you. I still am. I'm not mad, just relieved you're okay."

He brightened, then frowned. "I thought Mr. Thompkins was nice at first. He gave me dinner. You just pull this thing and the dinner gets hot all by itself. And it had dessert and everything."

"Better than tortillas and peanut butter, eh?" she asked, forcing herself not to imagine the boy exposed to the craziness in Bill Thompkins.

"Much better," Enrique agreed. "But I got scared of him when he made me hide in that cave. He said you wanted to hurt me. That you were mean to me."

She slid to the ground and pulled the boy onto her lap, ignoring the pain from the madman's cat claw scratches as the child nestled against her. "I would never want to hurt you," she said, and felt tears well in her eyes. She *had* hurt him. Not physically, but sometimes the withholding of affection could be far worse than a blow.

She thought of Daggert, how he'd ignored her at the start of their search, how he'd given her everything she could possibly want after that.

She looked around for him and spied him at the base of the clearing, checking Belle's legs and hooves. He moved to Enrique's horse, Dandelion, and did the same.

"My parents are dead, aren't they?" Enrique asked. "They weren't really taken by aliens."

"I'm afraid so, honey," she said, holding him close, drinking in the child smell of him.

"I wanted them to be alive."

"I know." She pressed her lips to his crown. "When my parents died, I looked for them everywhere. Like you, I even ran away a couple of times."

"You? But you never do anything wrong."

She smiled wryly. "Nobody's perfect."

"But you...you are," he mumbled into her shirt.

"No. If I were perfect, you never would have felt the need to run away."

"I didn't run away from you," he said, struggling to sit erect so he could meet her eyes. The earnest expression in his dark brown eyes let her see how true his statement was. "I just wanted to see my mama again."

"Oh, honey," Leeza said, and hugged him close, aching for him and, at the same time, feeling as if a huge weight had fallen from her shoulders.

Thompkins yelled out, "I need a doctor. Where's a doctor?"

Enrique shivered and huddled even closer. He whispered, "Mr. Thompkins is crazy, isn't he?"

Leeza chuckled. "As a bedbug."

"Why does he want to hurt people?"

Why did anyone want to hurt others? she wondered, and felt a stab of guilt for all the cutting things she'd said over the years, all the distance she'd placed between her and those who worked for her, worked with her. For all the children she'd hardened her heart against, not because she didn't like children, but because she was afraid of liking them too much and letting them glimpse her vulnerability.

It was impossible to love and not be vulnerable, she thought with sudden clarity. It wasn't a precept she would ever have been able to ponder before this remarkable journey; she would have had no frame of reference by which to identify the emotions or the single word that changed everything.

She did now.

She rocked Enrique and studied Daggert.

He'd finished checking Belle and Dandelion and was talking softly with Jack Dawson. She saw him glance in her direction, and go still when he realized her eyes were upon him. Then he deliberately returned his gaze to Jack.

She didn't know what it meant, but with Enrique in her arms, the sun warming her back and Daggert safe, albeit a little worse for the wear, she was content to wait.

With the exception of Jack Dawson, who stayed behind to watch over Bill Thompkins, they all went down the mountainside to the meadow far below. Enrique rode in front of Leeza on Belle, and Sancho happily danced from rock to trail, his bushy brown tail a gaily waving flag. Daggert rode Dandelion, but kept a hand on Belle's bridle, and if his face was a little paler than usual and his left arm looked odd in the sling Jack Dawson had made for him out of Leeza's ruined jacket, he still looked every bit the rock-hard carving of a man she'd originally thought him.

He still hadn't met her eyes. Except for that brief and poignant touch on the ledge, when he'd slid his hand beneath her wet hair and pressed his lips oh so tenderly to her forehead, calling her by the Apache name he'd given her, he hadn't shown her any indication that he was even aware she was still on the mountain.

Stone was waiting for them in the meadow. He managed to look embarrassed, as if he'd deserted the army just at the moment of battle. But he perked up when he spied Daggert, whickering and shaking his great head.

Once they'd dismounted, Daggert caught his horse's reins and murmured something to him. Stone pawed at the ground and tossed his head up and down. He gave a couple of prancing steps and rolled his liquid eyes.

Sancho threw himself into the grassy meadow and tumbled about, as if shedding any taint of the cliff side from his sable coat.

And Daggert smiled, watching his animals play. But the smile had a haunted quality that made Leeza's heart stumble. What was going through his head?

The helicopter arrived before she could ask him, and then, with all the commotion, she couldn't say anything personal.

A paramedic ran up the mountain, carrying a portable gurney. Jack Dawson would help him bring the wounded Thompkins back down.

Chance Salazar stepped from the chopper and, in a ducking run, came to join Leeza and Enrique. He stopped just shy of them, his eyes shadowed with worry, and looked as though he wanted to grab her, but instead held out his hand.

Leeza ignored the hand and stepped straight into her friend's husband's arms. She could feel his surprise as he hesitated before clasping to her with a firm, sure grip.

"You had us plenty worried, Leeza," he drawled into her ear.

She could see why Jeannie loved the man so. He was tall, warm and as solid as a brick wall. Leeza's eyes filled with tears. She had a lot to make up for, she thought. A lot of moments to recapture.

"Thanks for coming for us," she said, holding on. As far as she knew, this was the first time she'd hugged this wonderful friend.

Anyone keeping track might have noticed that she'd clung to Daggert, then to Enrique and now to Chance. It was a Leeza Nelson record. She smiled and let Chance go.

He studied her carefully and used the tip of a finger to tilt her chin, so as better to view the marks Thompkins had left on her cheek. "You okay?"

She smiled. "Just a scratch," she quipped.

He shook his head, released her and bent over Enrique. "And you, little Ricky. You are *so* grounded."

Enrique grinned up at him, wholly unafraid of him. None of the children were fearful around Chance. "Leeza came for me," he said.

Chance gave her an amused glance. "That she did, son."

"And she rides pretty good now," Enrique confided. "You shoulda seen her galloping straight for the caves. Just like in a movie. And then she jumped off right onto the cliffs."

Chance straightened and gave her a somewhat bemused smile. "I wish I had seen it," he said. And looked as though he meant it.

Leeza blushed. "It wasn't quite that smooth," she said.

"It was, honest," Enrique insisted.

Chance ruffled his hair and moved on toward Daggert. The two men spoke in lowered tones, their voices not carrying across the grassy field. Finally Chance made a cursory inspection of Daggert's gunshot wound. The two men clasped hands and Chance raised his free hand to Daggert's good shoulder, squeezing it tightly.

They all heard Thompkins's protests before they saw him being pulled into the meadow on the gurney-turned-travois the paramedic and Jack Dawson had attached to Thompkins's horse.

The paramedic applied an ointment to Leeza's scratches, adding a few butterfly bandages to a couple of deeper gouges on her chest and belly. He did the same for Daggert, then treated the gunshot wound.

Seeing Daggert in the sunlight, his naked torso shimmering golden, Leeza felt her mouth go dry and her limbs languorous.

The paramedic pronounced the wound serious and quickly bound his shoulder with pads and adhesive tape. He handed Daggert the remainder of the roll of tape and deftly fashioned a sling. "I'd tell you to get to a hospital, but you wouldn't do it, would you?"

Daggert didn't bother to answer and Leeza knew it was only his superb physical condition that would save him.

Thompkins was loaded in the helicopter first. Chance secured him to the bed with the safety straps and finished by effectively hog-tying his prisoner with an intricate series of interlocking hand-and-foot chains. And Leeza heard him tell the man that if he said so much as one single word, he'd gag him as well.

Thompkins began to cry, but didn't speak.

Leeza and Enrique got in next, and John Jenkins, who had a large footprint on the back of his jacket, followed, and finally the paramedic. Chance hopped into the copilot's seat and slammed the door shut. He gave the pilot a nod.

The man started the chopper's blades whirling, while Leeza cried out for them to wait for Daggert. Before Chance even spoke, she understood the significance of the paramedic's handing Daggert the medical supplies. Daggert wasn't coming with them.

"Someone's got to take the horses down," Chance called over the screeching wail of the helicopter blades.

"But he's been hurt," she yelled.

"He wants to do it," Chance said, his face serious and his eyes never leaving hers. "And Jack's riding with him."

"But we're out of food," Leeza said.

"We brought him some rations," Chance said. "They'll be okay."

"But—" And she saw the finality in the lawman's set mouth. He'd argued with Daggert about it, undoubtedly wanting to perform the task himself.

"He needs the time," Chance said.

He needed to find a bridge to the future, she thought. He needed time to let go of four years of vengeance. He needed time to mourn Donny without the anger that had kept him moving.

Three days. It would take three days to bring the horses down off the mountain.

"Wait," she said, leaping for the door. She fumbled with it for a few heart-breaking seconds before it sprang open, nearly spilling her to the grass below.

The whirling blades seemed mere inches above her and whipped her hair into her eyes. "Sancho," she called.

The dog heard her even over the roar of the helicopter.

"Here, Sancho. Come here, boy."

The dog eyed her questioningly, took a step in her direction, then looked back at Daggert for permission.

Daggert flinched as some unspoken emotion seized him. But he lifted his hand and waved toward the helicopter. Sancho shot across the meadow and leaped into the aircraft in one fluid bound.

He wagged his tail at Enrique. Grinned at Leeza. And sniffing, growled at Thompkins.

The paramedic helped her close the door, shutting out the two men in the meadow—the former lawman who hadn't believed Daggert four years earlier, but who stood by him now, and the tracker who had saved her life.

Chapter 14

Leeza understood how her friends must have felt when she was out on the mountain for three days; the time was interminable. Each hour passed at a maddeningly slow crawl. The sun rose too early, set too late, and when overhead, seemed to hang there forever.

The moon hung lopsided and low in the star-studded night and taunted her with its unhurried journey across the sky. It made her sleep fitful and restless and she longed for the deep sleep she'd found in the mountains, in the arms of the man she was waiting for.

She didn't know how many hours she stood with Sancho on the veranda, the handsome dog panting at her side while she squinted toward the west, hoping to see two tired men and four horses come riding in.

Her friends had gathered around her that first night, and soon everyone at Rancho Milagro had packed on to the veranda to pelt her with questions about the journey, about Daggert, about the man who used to work at Annie's Café. All the children had tales about him—his many weirdnesses, his snide manner. And all the adults were oversolicitous, hovering around Leeza as if she'd been diagnosed with a rare form of cancer.

She felt as if she had a disease, all right, but one that could only be cured by the sight of one rigid tracker on his big horse.

The second day, all but the children began to go about the routine tasks of maintaining the orphan's home. The children stayed with her, eyeing her candidly, overtly curious about the changes they sensed in her. And Enrique and Sancho never left her side, except to eat or sleep. Sancho wouldn't leave her even then.

By the morning of the third day, only she and Sancho sat vigil on the empty veranda, eyes trained on the western horizon.

In the way of New Mexico Septembers, the weather had turned cold and another storm was brewing in the mountains. The dawn had bloomed red and angry. And Leeza had felt tears stinging the back of her eyes.

In midafternoon, a truck kicked up a cloud of dust diving down the long ranch road, and Leeza stood, her heart beating with an almost painful dread. The ranch Labradors barked and raced around the yard. Sancho pressed against Leeza's leg.

When the dust cloud cleared and the pickup

stopped, a broad-faced, dark-skinned, solemn woman stepped down and went around to the passenger door. She opened it for a little girl of about two who looked like every lovely drawing of a Native American cherub. The woman lifted her down from the seat and hitched her to her waist.

She stopped when she saw Leeza in the shade on the large front veranda. "I am Alma TwoFeathers. You are Leeza Nelson?"

Leeza nodded. This was Daggert's wife? *Ex*-wife.

"They told me in town that you went into the mountains with James to find the man who killed my Donny."

Leeza shook her head, not knowing how to correct the woman. She felt wary and pierced with sorrow concurrently.

The woman's eyes dropped to the dog at Leeza's side and widened slightly. Then she smiled, and the expression transformed her face into one of rare beauty. Leeza struggled against a fierce stab of jealousy. This woman had shared Daggert's childhood, his culture, his bed. And his son.

"I came out here to say thank you," Alma said.

The jealousy left her as abruptly as it had arrived. "I didn't—"

The smiling woman interrupted her. "Doreen, down at the post office, told me that you saved the little boy who ran away. And how you saved James's life, too."

Leeza shook her head. Doreen was the local gossip and a brassy delight. But she had it wrong this time.

It hadn't been that way at all. "It was Daggert who saved me," she said honestly.

Alma studied her and, after a silent appraisal, nodded. "Good." She turned back to the pickup.

"Wait," Leeza said. "Would you like some iced tea? Or something else?"

Alma slowly turned around, her dark eyes steady, like those of the toddler she held in her arms. "No, I have to get back to the reservation to make dinner. Tell James that we'll have a sing for Donny next week. My husband has brought in a cacique. James hasn't come to any in the last four years. This time, I think maybe he will."

"I'll tell him," Leeza said, mystified.

"It will bring him peace."

Leeza's heart constricted. She didn't know what a cacique was or what a sing might be, but if it would bring James Daggert any measure of peace, she was all for it. She thought of the way he'd chuckled in her embrace, the way his voice rasped in his passion. But it wasn't peace.

"Well, goodbye," Alma said, and deposited her daughter back into the pickup and fastened her seat belt.

They were gone almost before the original dust cloud had fully settled.

Sancho barked, perhaps in farewell.

Leeza resumed her chair and stroked the dog's silky ears.

"He'll come," she said. "We just have to be patient."

* * *

Daggert pulled Stone to a halt at the Rancho Milagro border.

He could feel Leeza calling him.

"Something wrong?" Jack asked.

Daggert looked at the ground, then at the man who had ridden with him for the past three silent days. "I'm going to let you take the horses on in," he said. "Can you manage both of them?"

"Hell, from here, they'd wander in on their own. No problem." Jack didn't say anything else for a minute, then said, "I take it you're going home."

Daggert thought about his house—the walls plastered with clippings, maps, notes, any scrap of information that might lead him to Donny's killer. Home? It had been command central for four long years.

"Yes," he said, and offered no explanation.

"We didn't talk about what happened four years ago," Jack said suddenly. "Not your boy's death, but the way I handled the investigation."

Daggert's stomach clenched. It took all his will to maintain eye contact with the man on the horse beside him. "It doesn't matter."

Jack said slowly, carefully, "To me it does. I was wrong and I'm sorry for it."

Daggert closed his eyes, staggered by the man's admission. Prior to Donny's death, he'd admired Jack Dawson. The man had always treated him squarely, never giving him the grief so common to those who worked law enforcement without any badge. And the man had never made him feel less of a man because he was Apache. *I was wrong and I'm sorry for it.*

Daggert opened his eyes to see Jack's outstretched

hand waiting for him. He took the older man's hand, palm to palm, and held on.

He looked at their clasped hands. "Jack…for what you did four years ago—trying to stop me from seeing my son that way. For what you did three days ago, and riding with me since…for all that, I will always thank you," he said. His voice sounded raw even to himself.

Jack cleared his throat and gave Daggert's hand a final pump before releasing it.

"Go on now, son. I'll make the explanations."

Daggert found himself smiling at the man.

Jack winked at him, tipped a finger to his cowboy hat and whistled to the horses. "You take it slow now, y'hear? There's stormy days ahead."

Daggert waited until he couldn't see them anymore before turning his horse away from Rancho Milagro and heading toward his empty little house on the outskirts of Carlsbad. A house that would seem so much emptier now than it had when vengeance had lived there with him.

He tried not to think of Leeza Nelson and her beautiful eyes and unknowingly warm heart. He tried not to remember the way she felt beneath him, around him. He tried to forget her smile and the sharp little comments that always made him want to chuckle.

He tried, but he failed miserably. Painfully. Because he remembered every nuance of her scent, her taste, her feel. He remembered each word she'd spoken, each silly or wonderful thing she'd said. Like Donny, she was carved on his heart.

He knew Leeza would be hurt by his absence, confused by his disappearance. But he was also sure she'd be hurt a lot worse if he took her with him on this journey to find his soul. Because that was a hard trek a man had to make alone.

"Go on now," he told Stone.

The big horse shook his head and stomped a large hoof, as if arguing with him, as if trying to tell his rider he was every kind of a fool. Daggert dug in his heels, and the big horse quit his recalcitrance and started forward, hanging his head low against the desert sand.

Daggert urged Stone to a canter, as if wanting to leave the memories of Leeza at the miracle ranch's property lines.

And still he heard her calling, *"Daggert!"*

Chapter 15

Two weeks had passed since Jack Dawson rode into Rancho Milagro alone, leading two extra horses by one of Daggert's hackamore ropes. And Leeza still couldn't shake the numbness that had invaded her body and mind.

Jack Dawson had told them the tracker was exhausted and had decided to head straight down the river to his home. But Jack hadn't met her eyes during his little speech, and when she'd seen him lock gazes with Chance, she'd known that he lied.

Daggert hadn't been exhausted, though he probably needed a month's sleep; he simply hadn't wanted to come to Rancho Milagro. And there could be only one reason for that: her presence there.

"If you see him," she'd said, "tell him his ex-wife was here and said that a cacique was coming and they were performing a sing for Donny next week. She thought he might like to know.''

Dawson had nodded and, in the midst of farewells, assured her he would relay the message to Daggert. ''Anything else?'' he'd asked.

''Tell him...no, never mind.''

''It takes some time to come down from a four-year search,'' he said in a voice so low that no one else could have heard his words.

She'd wanted to believe Jack. She'd clung to his words for the next several days. She watched the waning moon and the later sunrises and earlier sunsets. She'd made popcorn for the children on a stormy night, and sat up with them while one of the cats delivered kittens.

But one day she gave up her spot on the veranda and coaxed Sancho to join her in her quarters. The dog seemed as listless as she felt. He whined in his sleep, his paws twitching, and she knew that, in his dreams, he ran for home, for Daggert.

She'd taken the silky coated dog as a pledge of security that the man would return to her.

But taking Sancho hostage had backfired. Daggert had done everything he'd vowed. He'd saved Enrique and he'd saved her. And he'd confronted his son's killer. She'd taken the dog so Daggert would come back for him. She'd taken Sancho hoping he'd come back for *her*.

But he hadn't.

Poor Sancho was as confused as she was, and as sad. But unlike her, he couldn't begin to understand why he'd been abandoned. And she couldn't explain it to him. She couldn't explain it to herself.

She heard a knock at the door to her quarters, a lovely three-room suite in the far eastern wing of the primary ranch headquarters.

"Come," she said.

Sancho didn't even lift his sable head or wag his bushy tail.

"Can I come in?" her friend Jeannie asked.

"Me, too?" Corrie added.

They rushed into her room as if anticipating her refusal. When had she ever refused either of them anything, except her confidences? And they'd had more of those than she ever shared with anyone else.

Jeannie sat down on Leeza's bed, while Corrie took the antique club chair by the window. They looked at her as if they carried bad news.

"What?" she asked, and felt her heart thud heavily. Something had happened to Daggert.

"Thompkins is going to trial at the end of the week," Jeannie said bluntly. "Chance wanted you to know. The prosecution expects you to testify."

"Fine," she said.

Corrie, elfin little creature that she was, tucked her bare feet beneath her in a seemingly impossible twist. She pushed a stray strand of chestnut hair behind her ear. Her eyes filled with tears. "What can we do?" she asked.

"About what?" Leeza looked away from the worry in her friend's eyes. Stay cool, she told herself.

"About the fact that your heart is breaking," Jeannie said matter-of-factly.

"Me? The shark without a heart?" Leeza asked, using one of her employees' favorite cracks about her.

Jeannie sighed and Corrie wiped her chocolate-brown eyes. Leeza dropped her gaze to the sorrowful dog at her feet.

"Okay, you want the truth?"

"Yes," Corrie breathed.

"Until I went after Enrique with James Daggert, I could have sworn everybody was right about me. I didn't have a heart, I had a lump of coal where my heart should be. Dr. Seuss met me before he wrote *The Grinch Who Stole Christmas*...the whole shebang. I was convinced that the reason Enrique ran away was because I was too hard on him."

"Oh, Leez," Jeannie said. But she exchanged a swift glance with Corrie.

Leeza smiled wryly. "You don't have to soft-pedal it. I *was* too hard. Every time I looked at him, I saw myself at that age, going from foster home to foster home and getting more hardened and more frightened with each one. By the time John and Cora Nelson took me in, I was a mess."

Jeannie's face tightened. She'd never said an unkind word about them—about anyone, to Leeza's knowledge—but her face now spoke volumes.

"Okay, they weren't the easiest people to cotton up to, as Chance would say. But they were doing the best they knew how, or at least what they believed was the right thing to do. And when I saw Enrique, I saw myself. I saw all his promise, and saw him throwing his chances away."

"But Enrique loves you," Corrie said.

Leeza studied her "little sister" and sighed. "Now, maybe. But he deserved more than I was dribbling out to him. He deserves the hugs, the kisses, the approbation, the everything I couldn't give him."

"But you can give it to him now," Jeannie said.

Leeza closed her eyes. "Exactly. Now. Because when I was out there on that mountain looking for him, a stranger showed me that I do have a heart."

"James Daggert," Jeannie said.

"As the only other choice was his horse or Bill Thompkins, yes, James Daggert."

"Do you love him?" Corrie asked.

Leeza remembered Daggert asking her that question about John and Cora.

She'd used James Daggert to find Enrique. He'd used her to find solace. They'd needed each other. And wanted each other. And she wanted him still. And ached for him. And found herself learning more about her own emotions every day because of him.

"Yes," Leeza said finally, and clenched her fist.

"Does he know?" Jeannie asked gently.

Leeza closed her eyes. "No. Not in so many words. At least, I never told him."

"It's not like you had a whole lot of time, hon," Jeannie said softly. "You were only out there three days."

"It was a lifetime," Leeza said, sighing. "I shouldn't have taken his dog. Sancho's miserable."

As if understanding the gist of the conversation, Sancho released a groan of resignation.

"Daggert will be at the trial," Corrie said hopefully, ever the optimist these days.

"Great. So what do I do—waltz up to him and declare my undying love? Say 'Sorry to bother you when you've made it perfectly obvious you don't want anything to do with me, but you brought me to life out there and I'm addicted to you now'?"

"Is that how you feel?" Jeannie asked.

Leeza looked out the window at the open grassland. "I don't know how I feel. I've never felt it before. Don't you get it? Until those three days with him, love was just a word, a symbol for something I didn't even understand. I feel like I've been colorblind all my life and everybody else was extolling the virtues of red, when all I could see was a dull gray."

Corrie slipped from the club chair and wrapped her arms around Leeza's neck. "It'll be okay."

Leeza patted her friend's arm and met Jeannie's eyes across the room. "Sure. There's nothing but sunshine and roses on the horizon."

Jeannie stood up. "James Daggert's ex-wife called this afternoon. She invited you to a sing for Donny this weekend."

Leeza straightened and extricated herself from Corrie's arms. "Another one? And what is that—a sing?"

"It's a cleansing ceremony," Jeannie said. "Anyone can do one, but sometimes they bring in a cacique, a medicine man, and he performs a highly stylized ritual. They call it a 'sing' because that's what the cacique does—he sings and chants until balance is restored."

"And I was invited?"

"Yes. She said to wear comfortable clothes, bring a coat and whatever you needed to stay overnight."

"I'll go," Leeza said. She felt a surge of hope. If nothing else, it would at least give her a glimpse of Daggert's world, the culture he'd grown up in, the place he called home.

"And she said to bring Sancho."

Leeza's heart fell. She heard it shatter on the hardwood floor.

Sancho growled, undoubtedly hearing it, too.

Daggert felt Leeza's presence before he saw her in the courtroom. He saw the heads turning, the sucking in of guts and the slack-jawed expression on the men's faces, and the straightening of shoulders and quick touches to their hair by the women.

But then, Daggert was sure that even if he were blind, he would know when Leeza Nelson entered a room. He would feel it.

As it was, it was as if the entire courtroom drew a stunned breath, shocked silent by her sheer beauty and command.

He turned finally and joined the crowd with his own swift intake of air. He'd seen her in fancy riding clothes, scruffy from the three-day ride in the desert, battered by a storm, naked in an icy river, and warm and glowing in their makeshift bed, but he'd never seen her in her eastern business garb. She was dressed all in cream, from her form-fitting suit to her cream heels, which made her taller than most men in the room. A single strand of pearls that Daggert had no doubt were real caressed her neck in the exact same place he remembered pressing his lips. Her blond hair was swept back in a loose, tousled style that Daggert was sure would soon be the most popular hairstyle in Carlsbad. And her cobalt eyes scanned the room with just a hint of disdain and condescension. A faint smile clung to her apricot-colored lips.

Lips that had met his with a passion such as he'd never encountered before. Lips that had served to wake him up as surely as the Prince had once woken Sleeping Beauty. Only in his case, it was Beauty who woke the heart-weary prince.

She saw him and, for a single heartbeat, checked her smooth entrance to the courtroom. She nodded coolly and her eyes moved beyond him. Dismissing him. He remembered her telling him that he could talk to her, that talking was surely in the great tracker rule book. He heard her tired voice asking him if he was enjoying himself when his hand had strayed too deeply beneath her blouse. And when he'd answered that he wasn't dead, she'd said that was something to look forward to.

She walked past him now, the sway of her skirt revealing her health, her beauty and her taunting of him.

Daggert smiled.

Leeza didn't look back at Daggert no matter how much she wanted to. She'd spent over an hour getting ready that morning, going through outfit after outfit, trying to decide just which article of clothing would drive him the most insane.

She always dressed with care, but never with such obsessive need to make a statement.

She'd wanted him to see that she was just fine. That the lack of a phone call or visit from a tracker from the wilds of New Mexico hadn't driven her out of her mind.

But when she saw him she almost forgot her determination to appear indifferent to him. Her heart had tried to leap from her chest as though seeking the one person who could make it pound so.

She'd never seen him in anything but jeans and Western wear suited to roughing it in the mountains. Standing there in a dark suit, his crisp white shirt a stark contrast to his earth-toned skin and jet-black hair, he stunned her with his sheer beauty. When they'd been out in the mountains, he'd reminded her of a lone black wolf. Strangely, with him in these formal clothes, stiffly standing there in a crowded courtroom, the image felt more accurate than ever.

She saw something in his eyes when he looked at her, but couldn't tell what it was. She'd given him a small nod and thought she caught the faintest glimmer of a smile. But she'd passed him by without waiting for that smile to deepen.

But she felt his eyes on her.

Don't burn yourself, she thought, and smiled at the memory.

As a material witness, she was only allowed in the courtroom during the opening session. The same rule applied to Daggert, but as they weren't supposed to confer on testimony, and she couldn't very well throw herself at his feet, she avoided him like the proverbial plague.

When she was called in for her testimony, she gave a concise account of her encounter with Bill Thompkins. She looked directly at the man who'd tried to kill Enrique, who'd shot Daggert and who had leaped down a cliff side and left deep gashes on her, and pointed him out to the interested jury.

No, she told the prosecutor, she hadn't known much about Bill Thompkins prior to her search for Enrique, only that he worked at Annie's Café. And yes, he'd frightened her. And yes, she'd believed he'd killed James Daggert. And no, she didn't believe any of them would have survived that day had Daggert not been alive, after all, and come after them to subdue Thompkins. Yes, Daggert had certainly helped the man to the ground, but kick him down? No. And as for the knife in the man's leg, she'd been the one to put it there, albeit unknowingly. She'd only been defending herself.

When the defense attorney asked her if she thought Thompkins had mental problems, she shrugged, disclaiming any pretensions to being an expert in the field of psychiatry.

"As a layman, Ms. Nelson, and a CEO who personally oversees the hiring and firing of a corporation employing more than three thousand workers, did you find something wrong with Bill Thompkins? Would you have hired him?"

Leeza frowned. "Hired him? Probably not. Fired him, almost certainly. I tend to terminate the employ of people who threaten to kill a nine-year-old boy and who strike at me with cutoff mountain lion paws. Call me silly, but I'd find that a pretty good rule to live by.''

At the nearly apoplectic response from the defense attorney, her candid statements were stricken from the record, but she knew the jury had heard them.

In truth, she agreed with little Enrique: the man was crazy. Did that make him above the law? She didn't believe so, but knew the way the indictment had been presented precluded any possibility that the man would be acquitted. He would either wind up in the state penitentiary, running from a nasty crowd of men who wanted to call him ''Sugar,'' or spend the rest of his days trading crayons with Napoleon and George Washington in an unpleasant state-run institution and doing the Thorazine shuffle. Either way he would be taken off the streets and out of the precious mountains that belonged to everyone, not just one psychopath who had animal fantasies.

She ran into Jack Dawson in the hallway, and though they didn't directly discuss the case, he let her know he'd persuaded the powers that be to reopen the investigation of Donny's murder.

Chance told her later that Jack's investigation revealed that DNA results conclusively proved the claws in Thompkins's possession were responsible for Donny's death. He also told her that Daggert had moved the jury to tears when he'd described what he'd seen on that mountain four years ago.

''And how was he?'' she asked, trying to sound casual.

''He was Daggert,'' Chance had said with a shrug. ''Not much ruffles that man.''

Leeza had wanted to argue with her friend's husband. Had, in fact, been angry with him for not seeing that such a description as Daggert had been requested to provide must have ripped his heart out and laid it on the evidence table for everyone to examine.

A lot ruffled Daggert.

Too much had. And for far too long.

What had Jack said—that shedding a four-year-long search took time?

She ran into Daggert on the way out of the courtroom the morning before the verdict came in. She was wearing a peach suit and he was wearing a gray blazer. The wolf in him seemed trapped, and obeying a compulsion she was helpless to fight, she crossed the foyer to lay a hand on his arm.

A war flared in his eyes, but no sign of it crossed his features.

''You did well,'' she said.

''Thank you,'' he answered, and looked as if he might say more. But just then a reporter shoved a microphone in front of his mouth and demanded to know if he thought the investigation into his son's death had been so delayed because he was Native American.

He lifted an arm against the microphone, his eyes sharp and angry.

''Be well,'' Leeza choked out, and turned away from him.

"Denzhoné…"

She stopped, tears filling her eyes.

But he said nothing else, and she let the crowd buffet her out the door.

Chapter 16

"How long will you be gone, Leeza?" Enrique asked her, leaning against the running board of the Chevy Avalanche she was driving to Ruidoso and the Mescalero Apache Reservation.

Leeza tossed her overnight bag into the jump seat and knelt down beside the boy. She dropped a hand on either side of his head, lightly gripping his thin shoulders. How naturally such a gesture came to her now. Only a month or so ago she hadn't known how to draw him onto her lap when he needed comfort; now small gestures of affection comforted them both.

"Only tonight, kiddo."

"And then you'll be back."

"I'm planning on it."

"I'll miss you," he said, and threw his arms around her neck, clinging fiercely and almost choking her.

She closed her eyes, relishing the sun-kissed scent of him, the sandy texture of his hair and her own ability to accept that unvarnished love and return it without hesitation.

She ruffled his hair as she stood up. She whistled for Sancho, who flew from the veranda into the front seat of the pickup's cab with a joyous bark.

"He's happy to go," Enrique said enviously.

Knowing the little boy ached to go with her, she said softly, "He hasn't been all that happy lately."

Enrique nodded and looked thoughtful. "That's because he doesn't know what's going on."

Leeza thought she wasn't faring any better than the dog.

"When will you be back?"

She sighed. Along with opening her heart to love, she'd opened it to a few other less pleasant emotions—like guilt. She unfastened her wristwatch and handed it down to the boy. "Can you tell time?" she asked.

He shook his head.

"Chance'll show you how," she said with an inner grin. "But what you need to know is that when this watch says the same thing it does right now—which is two o'clock—and when the sun is in the same spot tomorrow as it is right now, I'll be home."

"Cool," he said. "Is this for keeps?"

It was an Omega watch and had come dear. But it was only a watch, and she was, after all, a very, very wealthy woman. It was the first time in all her years of struggling to stay at the top of the venture capital game that she actually acknowledged the truth of her status, and the very first time she'd ever felt any enjoyment about it. It was only money. And spending it could be fun. She chuckled. "Sure, kiddo. Like us. We're for keeps, too."

The drive to the mountains was accomplished in less than two hours. It was hard to imagine that it had taken Daggert and her three days of hard riding to locate Enrique on the backside of this same mountain range. But then, they'd been following his trail from the ranch, and now she was driving a high-powered Chevrolet on a four-lane highway.

Sancho sat on the front passenger seat of the pickup, his face turned forward, grinning at the road stretching in front of them. As if he knew he would be seeing Daggert soon.

Leeza couldn't think of any other reason that Alma TwoFeathers would have requested the dog's presence at a ceremony to restore balance, except to return Sancho to his master.

Nervousness fluttered in Leeza's stomach and she drew a deep breath to steady herself. There was a slim possibility she would be seeing Daggert soon, as well. She hadn't seen him since the day before Bill Thompkins's verdict was announced.

She hadn't gone to the courtroom to hear that the man had been sentenced to life without parole in a mental institution for the criminally insane. The news accounts focused on his macabre actions and the more gruesome details of young Donny Daggert's death four years earlier. Leeza hoped Daggert hadn't listened to them, had been outside brushing Stone or walking in the foothills, soaking up peace.

Investigations were ongoing—the hiker, the house-wife, the couple who had been necking in their car. In fact, most of the area's accidental-death cases and all of the animal-mauling cases had been reopened and were being thoroughly cross-checked.

Following Alma TwoFeathers's directions—which consisted of such oddities as "turn south at the big tree with two dead branches on the top of the hill" and "when you see the rock that looks like a moose, turn west" —and stopping for help at least four times, Leeza finally pulled up in front of a bright pink house nestled among tall pines.

Six or seven other cars were parked haphazardly around the unfenced yard. A pot of straggling mums sat near the front steps, the only colorful relief to an otherwise monotone expanse. Several dogs of varying breeds ran around her pickup barking happily.

Sancho barked back eagerly.

Alma TwoFeathers appeared on the top step, hold-ing the little girl that looked so much like her that Leeza was easily able to picture the baby as a grown woman with a babe of her own.

Leeza rested her hand on her flat stomach, willing her nerves to behave. Was this newfound nervousness also a by-product of finding her heart? When it had been missing, unlooked for, she'd done or said any-thing she pleased, and was never nervous. Was that because compunction, respect, the need for approba-tion—these made one afraid of hurting someone or being hurt in return?

"I'm glad you came," Alma said, her flat voice scarcely changing inflection. Nor did her expression alter one iota until she spied Sancho in the front seat. Then she smiled a little. "It's good you brought the dog."

Leeza approached her for a quick handshake. "Thank you for inviting me."

"The others are not here yet. Only some of my family. You can let the dog out of the car. He knows the others."

Leeza did so, and Sancho bounded from the car with an enthusiasm he hadn't shown in the past three weeks. She shouldn't have stolen him from Daggert.

"Come inside. I'm making food."

Leeza was reminded of some of the simplistic things Daggert had said during their journey. Of the river they'd bathed in, made love beside, he'd said it was a tributary. *Some are big, some are small.*

But he'd also said, "Nothing's simple."

She didn't know what she expected as she crossed the threshold of the TwoFeathers home, but once inside, felt she'd stepped into another country. The interior was different from anything she'd ever seen before. Old and well-worn sofas and chairs lined the walls in stark symmetry, with no attention to the modern practice of feng shui. Two pictures hung on the wall, one a print of a horse, the other a painting of Jesus Christ. A large-screen television dominated the far wall of the small living area, and four children sat inches away from it, staring at the picture with an intensity just shy of hypnotized. Wile E. Coyote hung in midair, turned to face them, waved goodbye and disappeared downward in a whoosh. The children giggled.

The place was permeated with the odor of beans, homemade tortillas and frying bread. Leeza's stomach rumbled.

"Come in the kitchen," Alma said, stepping over the children on the floor. Leeza followed, doing the same. The children never looked at them.

Three women all but filled the small kitchen nook. Though varying in age and size, each of them resembled Alma, with the same dark eyes, broad face, and perfectly even white smile that shone to such advantage against her dark complexion.

Each of the women was busily engaged in a different task—one rolling tamales, swiftly pressing a red-chili meat mixture into a moist corn dough and rolling it in a corn husk; another stirring a pot of *posole,* a hominy-pork-and-green-chili stew that smelled heavenly. The eldest was tossing a round of dough in deft fingers, creating a large, perfect tortilla.

"These are my sisters, Angie and Doris, and my mother, Nina."

Leeza couldn't tell which were her sisters and which was Alma's mother; they all looked too close in age for one to be the grandmother of the baby on Alma's hip. She smiled and nodded and admitted her confusion.

Alma smiled back while the other women giggled. "These are my sisters-in-law you would say. They are my husband's mother's family and now mine."

She must have caught a question on Leeza's face, for she added, "James's mother, who is Apache, became my mother when we were married. We never knew his father, but it doesn't matter. James will always be of the tribe.''

''And his children?'' Leeza couldn't help asking.

Alma met her gaze with a mischievous look. ''Always.''

''This is the woman I was telling you about,'' Alma announced warmly to her family. ''Her name is Leeza.''

There were smiles all around and many nods, and soon they had Leeza chopping tomatoes, shredding cheese and peeling green chilis.

If Daggert could find peace anywhere, she thought, wiping the streaming tears from her eyes from the sting of the chili, and grinning at the teasing women, it would be in this warm kitchen with the rich smells, the laughter and the simple hard work of preparing a feast.

Daggert froze in the doorway of the living area, watching Leeza Nelson in his ex-wife's kitchen, laughing at something his former mother-in-law had said.

He'd seen the new pickup in the driveway, but hadn't connected it with Rancho Milagro. He'd only wondered that the dogs were off somewhere, chasing up rabbits or squirrels, when there were so many good smells emanating from the house.

He hadn't wanted to come tonight, but with all that had happened in the last few weeks, he knew it was time to set things right in his heart. And the cacique Alma's husband had brought in was a powerful one and one of the oldest in the country.

In a million years, Daggert would never have expected to find Leeza Nelson there, laughing in the kitchen with two women who barely spoke English and two others who had shared about as much contact with the white world as Leeza had with the Apache.

"Uncle James!" one of the children cried, and leaped up from the floor. The others did the same, and over the general chaos of him struggling to hold four children at once, Leeza looked his way and their gazes locked.

Her eyes, still moist from her laughter or from her battle with the green chilis before her on the cutting board, seemed huge and so incredibly blue that he felt a jolt of sharp recognition in his heart. He'd seen her with tears on her cheeks, her eyes luminescent and shimmering with unshed pain. And he'd seen them wet in the aftermath of her release.

The children clambering over him, slowly slid down his body, sensing something different about him, feeling the tension in the room.

The females in the kitchen studied the white woman in their midst, who was suddenly still, and their eyes slowly traveled from Leeza to James Daggert.

He suspected Leeza didn't see their exchange of glances or Alma's swift nod and secretive smile, but he did.

"*Dáoté,* James," Alma said, welcoming him in Apache.

"*Dáoté,*" he said absently, unable to take his gaze from the sight of Leeza in this kitchen.

He was pleased to note that her hands were trembling. She'd seemed so cool and collected in the courthouse, except for that one moment when he'd called her by his private name for her. And even then she'd only stiffened before walking away.

She looked much more approachable in the warm kitchen, with her tousled hair slightly damp from the heat, her elegant but casual clothes steamed a bit, and her eyes linked with his. Her lips parted and he knew he would die if he didn't taste them that night.

"Well, come in," his former mother-in-law said. "You must be hungry. Take a plate and eat."

It wasn't the Apache way to sit down to a formal meal. When someone was hungry, he or she took food. It was simple.

He picked up a paper plate and began dipping into the various pots to explore the feast. Stepping around the still-working women, he took a couple of steamed tamales, a bowl of *posole,* a chunk of seasoned brisket and, brushing against Leeza, a handful of her freshly chopped vegetables.

She stilled again when his arm reached around her, and stiffened as he leaned his body against her back. And sighed when his breath tickled the nape of her neck. He would have kissed her right there had they been alone. And his loins reacted with sharp need.

He pulled away from her and slowly made his way back to the living area. One of Alma's new sisters-in-law giggled as he passed her. He felt a flush staining his cheeks a deeper red than they were already. But his own lips twitched.

Just being in the same small house with James Daggert made her body come alive. Her heartbeat was lighter, her breathing shallower, her senses heightened. Her breasts seemed fuller, her legs silkier, her hair touchable, and her lips ached for the feel of his.

The house continued to accrue people until there wasn't a single seat left and nowhere to move except around the various pots and platters of plentiful food. The television continued to blare, though no one seemed to be watching it.

The children—by now their ranks had grown to more than twenty—were playing some game in the front yard that required a great deal of screaming and running with the pack of dogs.

Old men with unbound, long white hair sat smoking cigarettes on the steps and old women with missing teeth and lovely wrinkled faces swapped dirty jokes—Alma had told Leeza—in Apache and giggled madly, slapping each other at the punch lines.

Alma's husband arrived last, bringing the medicine man, the cacique.

Leeza studied the man Alma had chosen to replace the vengeance-driven Daggert. At first glance, he seemed the antithesis of Daggert. He was short by any standard, scarcely coming to Leeza's breasts, and sported a barrel chest that continued straight to his thighs. His dark hair was short and his face round, his eyes black. But when he spoke, she heard a thread of similarity—a quiet silken tone that seemed to caress his new wife and express a deep pride in his little girl.

The cacique was probably the oldest man Leeza had ever met in her life. Like Alma's husband, he was short, but there was nothing diminutive about him. He radiated peace and concern. He touched women, men, children. And held Leeza's hand for a long time, searching her eyes as if looking directly into her soul. Like Daggert, he could read her. Instead of making her uncomfortable, she smiled at the old man.

He smiled back and patted her hand.

"Denzhoné Bidáá," she heard Daggert telling the old man some time later. She asked Alma why Daggert would tell the cacique the name he'd given her.

Alma looked at her for a long while before smiling. "He wants the cacique to sing a song for you."

To restore balance, Leeza thought. To say farewell.

"Will he do that for anyone?" Leeza asked Alma. Alma shrugged.

"Can you teach me a phrase in Apache?" She no longer found it strange to be talking so intimately and easily with Daggert's ex-wife. Alma and Daggert had been childhood friends, were friends still and had shared Donny. They had family and culture in common.

"What phrase?"

Leeza told her.

Alma looked surprised, and her eyes shifted to Daggert, far across the room, before returning to Leeza. She smiled and nodded. "Like this. *Hidłoh N'deen.*"

Shortly before Alma's husband herded everyone outside to a roaring fire he'd built in the side yard, away from the pine trees and cars, Leeza approached the old cacique.

She haltingly made her request and was relieved when he didn't shake his head. He corrected her pronunciation and patted her hand, walking away muttering, pulling his long, colorful wool blanket around his shoulders.

Leeza had expected a solemn, perhaps dolorous ceremony with many rituals she wouldn't be able to follow. Instead, the crowd of some fifty people easily formed a loose circle around the roaring blaze and either sat or stood around with drinks in their hands or smoking cigarettes. The cacique sat on a sawn log at the westernmost edge of the circle, slightly in front of the others. A couple of other men joined him, sitting directly on the earth. They set large deer hide drums on their sinewed sides, their drinks away from danger of tipping over, and began striking the drums with long, hand-hewn drumsticks.

The sound was hollow and resonant and quieted the rowdy crowd somewhat.

The cacique began chanting in Apache, his old man's voice strong and sure in his atonal singing.

Daggert slipped behind Leeza and breathed a translation in her ear.

"The stars shine down on these people.
The stars are our brothers.
The stars keep the deer safe for us.
The stars show us the way home.
Good are the stars.
Good are our brothers."

His warm breath played on the sensitive skin beneath her ear, mingling with the cacique's song and the sweet meaning.

Unconsciously, she leaned back against him, and, at the contact, sighed and felt she'd finally come home. She belonged in this man's arms. Belonged to him in a way she could never fully understand nor wanted to analyze. His arms wrapped around her and sheltered her from the chill late September air.

The cacique continued to chant with the beat of his drummers. Daggert's hot breath returned to her throat.

"The moon shines down on these people.
The moon is our mother.
The moon keeps the elk safe for us.
The moon shows us the way home.
Good is the moon.
Good is our mother."

Leeza let her head loll against Daggert's broad shoulder, savoring the feel of him, aching to feel even more, his velvet voice as seductive as his eyes and luring her deeper into love for him.

The drummers stopped, but she could still feel Daggert's heart beating against her. It was the rhythm of the drums, she thought. A perfectly natural rhythm that echoed man's heartbeat, the heartbeat of the earth.

The cacique drank a sip of coffee and began chanting again.

Leeza waited for Daggert's translation and turned her head to look at him when he didn't whisper in her ear. His face was as closed as his tightly shut eyes.

She didn't have to ask for the meaning; she knew it was about Donny.

But then Daggert's lips moved and he said against her cheek,

"A man and a woman followed their brothers.
A man and a woman followed their mother.
A man and a woman went on a big quest.
The quest was important.
Their brothers and their mother helped them.
Their cousins, the wind and rain, helped them.
A man and a woman found what they were look- ing for.
Good to have brothers, a mother and many cous- ins."

Daggert finished his translation by pressing his lips against her cheek.

She made an almost inaudible sound of acceptance and he lowered his lips to the hollow of her throat, grazing her collarbone with slow, warm hunger.

The cacique swallowed another sip of his coffee and signaled the drummers to begin anew. The beat was faster this time, and Leeza realized it once again matched their heartbeats exactly.

Several cheers went around the circle and the cacique waved Daggert and her forward. Thinking this might be a thank-you for searching for Donny's killer, half afraid she would have to do something and, in her inexperience, spoil the ceremony, Leeza clung to

Daggert's hand as he led her forward until they stood near the cacique.

The old man motioned for them to sit down. Someone brought a large blanket and handed it to Daggert. He looked at it for a long moment, then at her. She suspected it had been Donny's. His lips quirked in a half smile that addressed some inner pain. Then he shook the blanket open and draped it around their shoulders. Beneath the blanket, he put his arm around her and drew her close. She rested her arms on his bent leg.

The cacique began to chant, and soon others in the circle were chanting with him. The drummers beat their instruments faster and faster and the crowd around the circle chanted louder and louder. The fire leaped into the air, showering sparks across the dirt. Children began dancing from foot to foot to the beat and were soon joined by many of the adults. Someone splashed beer over Daggert and Leeza's heads.

The drummers stopped and the cacique's song seemed to linger in her ears even as the crowd cheered.

Whatever the song meant, it was obvious it lifted everyone's spirits and was cause for celebration.

Not taking the blanket from their shoulders, Daggert raised them up in a fluid motion. To the crowd's satisfaction, he kissed her.

To the crowd's delight, she kissed him back.

Chapter 17

Daggert didn't translate the cacique's last song for Leeza. Her sparkling eyes and smiling lips let everyone believe she knew what had been chanted in her name. Using her name.

It was all he could do to drag his lips from hers amid cheers from his cousins, friends and their families. But he didn't let her go. He folded her elegant hand in his and held her close to his side as the sing broke up.

He felt released and born anew.

Maybe if he'd come to one of the sings anytime these past four years, he would have felt better, but he didn't believe it. It had taken three perfect days with Leeza and the capture of his son's murderer to allow him to seek the peace that used to live within him.

If he'd come to one of the sings, he'd have been accompanied not by a beautiful woman with mountain water in her eyes, but an angry, writhing vengeance. And he would have resisted the chanting that might have driven it away.

Alma approached them, carrying her little girl. He suspected she was pregnant again because she'd taken on that radiance some women adopted when new life quickened inside them.

"James, I'm happy for you," she said, meeting his eyes directly.

He gave her a tender kiss on her upraised cheek and flicked the sleeping baby's tiny nose. "And I for you, Alma. Thank you."

Alma turned to Leeza and pulled the blanket a little tighter around the blond woman's shoulders. "I'm glad you came tonight," she said formally.

"Me, too," Leeza said, smiling that dazzling smile that lit her eyes and stole his breath.

"The cacique is staying with us. We've arranged for you to stay at the Tsotses's house down the road. James knows the way there. Okay?"

"That's wonderful," Leeza said. "Thanks again."

A smile flickered across Alma's normally stoic features. "Until tomorrow." She turned away, then called back over her shoulder, "And take your dog with you, James. He doesn't like sleeping outside and I won't have dogs in the house."

Daggert was stunned. "You brought Sancho with you?"

Leeza looked surprised. "Alma told me to." She averted her gaze. "I thought…"

"What did you think, *Denzhoné?*"

She lifted her face, and without avoiding his eyes, said, "I thought you must want him back and didn't want to see me."

That it took grit to get the words out was obvious. That it took guts to reveal so much of her hurt didn't surprise him, however, because she had more innate courage than any other person he'd ever met.

"I wanted to see you," he said. "I just didn't dare until I cleared some things up. Things that had been hanging on too long."

"It hurt," she said.

"Come," he said. "Let me take you to Tsotses's place."

She hung back. "Will they be there?"

"No. They moved away a long time ago. Everybody uses it as a guest house now."

She chuckled. "This is all pretty alien to me, you know."

"The mountains were alien to you, but you learned quickly."

She allowed him to lead her to the shiny new Chevy Avalanche, her arm around his waist, her other hand clinging to the blanket surrounding both of them. By the time they made it to the pickup, he was sure that everyone at the sing, the cacique included, had managed to slap him on the back or pat Leeza's shoulder. Babies reached out for her gold hair and dogs buffeted their legs.

Alma's mother pressed a sack filled with food into his hands and kissed him soundly. "*Shegoneh,*

James,'' she said, formally bidding him farewell. ''And you I will see again,'' she said to Leeza.

Daggert assisted Leeza into the passenger's seat and took the keys from her. ''Do you trust me?'' he asked, meaning to drive.

''With my life,'' she said solemnly. But a wicked light danced in her lovely eyes.

Leeza thought the Tsotses's house was identical in style to the TwoFeathers's home except it was painted a strident candy-apple green and more flowers had survived the early cold and were blooming haphazardly in the beds closest to the front door.

She waited as Daggert opened the door without a key and flicked on the lights. A single, overhead bulb lit the same floor plan as the TwoFeathers's home, and like Alma's, the furniture was arranged with every chair's back against a wall. And while the television was considerably smaller, the room seemed dominated by it.

Sancho raced ahead of them, great tail wagging, bounding from room to room with delighted discovery. In each new room, which proved to be two beyond the living room and kitchen combination, he barked at Leeza as if asking her to check it out for herself.

She smiled as Daggert held a bowl over the kitchen sink, filled it with water and set it down for the dog before turning back to her. He paused and she was reminded of the day he'd groomed Belle so thoroughly and she had imagined those gentle hands roaming her own body.

She shivered beneath the blanket she still wore, not from cold, but from sheer anticipation.

He crossed the room as slowly and deliberately as he'd forded the river.

Her knees felt weak. Her breath came and went in short, light gasps. She felt dizzy and languorous.

He took her in his arms in a contemplative, deliberate embrace, but even as she tilted her head up for his kiss, he paused. "I'm sorry for hurting you, *Denzhoné*. It was the last thing I wanted to do."

Her heart beat painfully in her chest. "Jack said it took time to wind up a four-year search."

Daggert smiled crookedly. "Jack said that? He was right."

"And are you finished?"

"Vengeance doesn't live in my house anymore," he said.

Daggert thought of the freshly painted walls, the stacks of papers and maps he'd turned over to the investigators researching the Thompkins case. And the new bed in his bedroom.

"And your heart, Daggert?" she asked—wistfully, he thought.

"Ah, my heart. That doesn't belong to me," he said.

She stilled in his arms. "No?"

"No. It belongs to you, *Denzhoné*."

He felt the relief sweep through her, and knew just how deeply he had hurt her. "Well, that seems only fair," she said, taking on a businesslike, considering expression.

"How's that?" he asked, smiling. He couldn't help

it, just holding her made him want to laugh out loud and shout her name to the stars. His brothers.

"You found mine. Before you, I didn't know for sure I even had one. So you found mine, then stole it. And I get yours."

He kissed her then, unable to resist her alluring lips, her smart, beautiful mouth. And felt he was dying from the hunger she roused in him. And made to live again in her heated response.

He felt her shake free of the blanket around her shoulders, and caught the brightly patterned wool before it hit the floor. "Come," he said, leading her to the larger of the two bedrooms.

He didn't bother finding the light, he merely left the door ajar, allowing the light from the living room to spill into the semidark bedroom. He drew open the curtains and let the moonlight cascade over the bed.

He dropped the blanket to the bed and gently pushed her down upon it. Without saying a word, he slowly unlaced her tennis shoes and pulled them from her arched feet. He slowly tugged her socks free and tossed them aside.

She smiled a little as his fingers unfastened the button at her waist and pulled the zipper down. He spread the flaps wide and ran his hands over her satin flesh, slipping beneath her blouse to caress her smooth skin.

She lifted her buttocks to help him slip the jeans from her long legs, and he heard her gasp as he pressed his lips to the sensitive skin just beside her knee.

He felt desperate to feel the warmth inside her, to

lose himself in her, but he wanted this night to be the most special of all nights and wanted her to never forget just how much she claimed of him, his whole heart. His whole body. And his soul.

Running his hands down the length of her legs, he hooked his forefingers in the elastic of her silken underwear and slowly pulled the wispy material down her legs, sending it flying somewhere, and making him groan at the lovely sight opening to him.

He unfastened his shirt buttons, unable to take his eyes from her stunning body. And smiled as her trembling fingers worked at the buttons of her blouse. He trembled himself as her eyes drank in the sight of his bared chest.

He tossed his shirt aside and unfastened his jeans.

Leeza started to sit up and he stopped her, holding her upright only long enough to push her blouse from her shoulders and unfasten her lacy bra. He gently deposited her back on the bed, watching the fire in her eyes, the desire coloring her smile.

He pulled his boots off and dropped them. From the kitchen, Sancho barked, and Leeza chuckled. It was a sound rich with humor, bubbling with desire.

Daggert pushed down his jeans and stepped out of them.

"In a minute, I'm going to stuff a ten dollar bill in your shorts," Leeza said, her voice choked with feeling.

He laughed and pushed down his shorts, kicking them aside. Out in the mountains, she'd made him feel like a god. With her cobalt eyes roaming his body, stroking him with her gaze, he felt more than that—he felt all-powerful, pure male strength.

And he'd found his perfect counterpart, pure female warmth.

He stepped to the bed and gently spread her legs and felt his breath catch at the sheer beauty beneath him. He ran his hands up her inner thighs and brushed the blond crown of hair at her apex. She moaned as he slowly kissed her there, finding that perfect nub of pleasure and teasing her with his tongue.

He stroked her soft, firm thighs, then lifted her legs to straddle his shoulders, and kissed her more deeply, tasting her, tormenting her. She writhed beneath him, making him shake with need for her. Kneading her rounded bottom, he slipped a finger into her molten core and groaned aloud as her inner muscles grasped him, pulling him deeper.

"Daggert," she cried. "Please…"

He didn't stop.

"Wait… I want you inside me, please," she begged, and her voice held such a raw note of longing that he was helpless to resist her siren call or the lure of her silken calves gliding down his back.

He ran a hand over his mouth and crawled up the bed between her glorious legs. He stopped to taste a hardened nipple and flick his tongue across her puckered aureole. And being a fair man, he couldn't let the other breast go without equal attention.

He scooped her golden-hued globes together and grazed his teeth over the nipples just inches apart.

"You're driving me crazy," she growled, arching up to grant even greater access.

He shifted higher and, poised over her, met her eyes for a long, heart-stopping minute. She raised a hand to his lips and traced them with a light fingertip. He kissed it. She trailed it down his throat and over his chest, continuing lower, until it met his full arousal. Touching the very tip, she tapped lightly, making him bounce against her.

"Ahh," he groaned. "You're playing with fire."

"Oh, but I like the heat," she purred.

He grabbed her hand away and moved it high above her head, pinning her wrist to the bed, and when she would have taken him with her other hand, did the same to her other wrist. He held them loosely trapped beneath his palm, and smiled when he felt her fingers curl around the heel of his hand.

"I've got you now," he said.

"As long as you like," she murmured, arching up to kiss him deeply.

He groaned into the kiss, his body aching for her, needing to meld with hers, his heart desperate to beat against hers.

"How about forever?" he asked, pulling back only to slide into her.

"Forever's good," she gasped, wrapping her legs around him and drawing him deeply into her.

"This is good," he said, rocking faster.

"This is definitely good," she agreed, pressing her breasts to his chest.

She was right, he thought. It was definitely good, but it was even more than that. "It's perfect," he murmured against her lips. "Because I love you, *Denzhoné*."

She ground against him, her body thrashing beneath his, and she cried out as a storm raged through her. "And I...love...*you!*" And she convulsed beneath him as the storm broke.

Her admission shattered his control. He drove into her with almost desperate hunger and exploded upon contact.

He continued rocking into her, loving her, the hunger in him sated, but the desire for her a continuous thrum in his very soul. And felt her contracting around him, holding him, taking every last drop of him.

Later, holding her against his chest, lulled nearly asleep by the intensity of their mutual passion, Daggert lightly, gently stroked her back. She raised her head a little and said his name.

"What did the cacique chant tonight? In that song about us?"

"Oh that," he said. He drew her back down to his chest and pressed his lips to her forehead. "It was a blessing."

"A blessing?"

He thought of the honest way she'd told him he'd hurt her. The honesty when she admitted she'd never climaxed with anyone before. The sincerity in her admission of love for him.

"It was a ceremony of marriage."

"A what?"

"Haven't you ever heard about the dangers of sitting under a blanket with someone?"

She gave a brief chuckle. "Not in relation to marriage, no."

"Well, now you know what they are."

"You're kidding me, right?"

"It's not legal in the white man's world."

He felt her go perfectly still. And held his breath, waiting for her response.

Finally, she said, "That's why you told him the name you gave me?"

"Yes."

"You wanted to marry me?"

"Yes."

"And in the other world?"

"There, too."

He felt her release a sigh and nestle closer to him. Was that an answer? He found himself holding his breath, hoping against hope.

"Are you asking me?"

"Yes."

"And will you promise to love me forever?"

"Yes."

"I thought you didn't believe in promises."

"I didn't," he said, smiling. "But I do now."

"Because you can't get me any other way."

"Because I can't live without you, *Denzhoné*."

"I have to be back at the ranch before two o'clock tomorrow."

"That's possible," he said. "But why?"

"Because of a promise I made to Enrique."

"And you always keep your promises," he said, turning her in his arms and meeting her beautiful, beautiful eyes.

"I do," she said.

"And so will I," he said solemnly, willing her to

believe him, to trust him. To know that he would always be there for her. With her.

"You know I'm rich," she said.

"I'm a tracker. I'm not stupid."

She chuckled.

"We'd probably have to live at Rancho Milagro."

"We could live on the moon for all I care," he said.

"It's a good place to raise children."

"It is that," he agreed, feeling a momentary pang of sorrow that she'd never known Donny, never would. "Why did you tell the cacique to call me Man Who Laughs?"

"Because you will always, always take my breath away."

Daggert kissed her and felt arousal kindle anew. She took him with sweet languor, riding him, claiming him as her own. Believing in him with every fiber of her being. He felt it. And he knew he touched the most vulnerable part of her when she called out his name as she climaxed, and sobbed her love for him in the shuddering aftermath.

She held him this time, cradling his head against her full breasts. She lightly brushed her fingers through his hair. She sighed.

"Tell me," he said.

"I was thinking that it's just as well we already got this wedding ceremony stuff out of the way."

He chuckled and nuzzled a breast. "Why is that, *Denzhoné?*"

She took his hand and placed it on her flat belly.

"Because I'm old-fashioned enough to believe that children need two parents, preferably married."

He jerked up to his elbow and stared down at her, his hand still on her, over the life she carried inside.

"You're sure?" he asked.

"Yes. Do you mind?"

He grabbed her in his arms and rolled her over on top of him, kissing her all the while. "Mind?" he asked, when he could bring himself to release her. "Mind? It's everything I ever could have hoped for."

She smiled tremulously at him.

"I have a confession," he said.

She blinked. "Another one? You've already gotten me pregnant, tricked me into marriage…what else is there?"

"I have a pretty hefty stock portfolio of my own."

She laughed out loud and he joined her.

"I love you, *Denzhoné Bidáá*…my lovely Leeza."

"And I you, Man Who Laughs."

And he did.

* * * * *

If you enjoyed what you just read,
then we've got an offer you can't resist!

Take 2 bestselling love stories FREE!

Plus get a FREE surprise gift!

Clip this page and mail it to Silhouette Reader Service™

IN U.S.A.
3010 Walden Ave.
P.O. Box 1867
Buffalo, N.Y. 14240-1867

IN CANADA
P.O. Box 609
Fort Erie, Ontario
L2A 5X3

YES! Please send me 2 free Silhouette Intimate Moments® novels and my free surprise gift. After receiving them, if I don't wish to receive anymore, I can return the shipping statement marked cancel. If I don't cancel, I will receive 6 brand-new novels every month, before they're available in stores! In the U.S.A., bill me at the bargain price of $3.99 plus 25¢ shipping and handling per book and applicable sales tax, if any*. In Canada, bill me at the bargain price of $4.74 plus 25¢ shipping and handling per book and applicable taxes**. That's the complete price and a savings of at least 10% off the cover prices—what a great deal! I understand that accepting the 2 free books and gift places me under no obligation ever to buy any books. I can always return a shipment and cancel at any time. Even if I never buy another book from Silhouette, the 2 free books and gift are mine to keep forever.

245 SDN DNUV
345 SDN DNUW

Name	(PLEASE PRINT)
Address	Apt.#
City	State/Prov. Zip/Postal Code

* Terms and prices subject to change without notice. Sales tax applicable in N.Y.
** Canadian residents will be charged applicable provincial taxes and GST.
All orders subject to approval. Offer limited to one per household and not valid to current Silhouette Intimate Moments® subscribers.
® are registered trademarks of Harlequin Books S.A., used under license.

INMOM02   ©1998 Harlequin Enterprises Limited

Your opinion is important to us! Please take a few moments to share your thoughts with us about your experiences with Harlequin and Silhouette books. Your comments will be very useful in ensuring that we deliver books you love to read. *Please take a few minutes to complete the questionnaire, then send it to us at the address below.*

Send your completed questionnaires to:
Harlequin/Silhouette Reader Survey, P.O. Box 9046, Buffalo, NY 14269-9046

1. As you may know, there are many different lines under the Harlequin and Silhouette brands. Each of the lines is listed below. Please check the box that most represents your reading habit for each line.

Line	Currently read this line	Do not read this line	Not sure if I read this line
Harlequin American Romance	❏	❏	❏
Harlequin Duets	❏	❏	❏
Harlequin Romance	❏	❏	❏
Harlequin Historicals	❏	❏	❏
Harlequin Superromance	❏	❏	❏
Harlequin Intrigue	❏	❏	❏
Harlequin Presents	❏	❏	❏
Harlequin Temptation	❏	❏	❏
Harlequin Blaze	❏	❏	❏
Silhouette Special Edition	❏	❏	❏
Silhouette Romance	❏	❏	❏
Silhouette Intimate Moments	❏	❏	❏
Silhouette Desire	❏	❏	❏

2. Which of the following best describes why you bought *this book?* One answer only, please.

the picture on the cover	❏	the title	❏
the author	❏	the line is one I read often	❏
part of a miniseries	❏	saw an ad in another book	❏
saw an ad in a magazine/newsletter	❏	a friend told me about it	❏
I borrowed/was given this book	❏	other: _____	❏

3. Where did you buy *this book?* One answer only, please.

at Barnes & Noble	❏	at a grocery store	❏
at Waldenbooks	❏	at a drugstore	❏
at Borders	❏	on eHarlequin.com Web site	❏
at another bookstore	❏	from another Web site	❏
at Wal-Mart	❏	Harlequin/Silhouette Reader	❏
at Target	❏	Service/through the mail	
at Kmart	❏	used books from anywhere	❏
at another department store or mass merchandiser	❏	I borrowed/was given this book	❏

4. On average, how many Harlequin and Silhouette books do you buy at one time?

I buy _____ books at one time	❏
I rarely buy a book	❏

MRQ403SIM-1A

5. How many times per month do you shop for any *Harlequin and/or Silhouette* books?
One answer only, please.

1 or more times a week	❏	a few times per year	❏
1 to 3 times per month	❏	less often than once a year	❏
1 to 2 times every 3 months	❏	never	❏

6. When you think of your ideal heroine, which *one* statement describes her the best?
One answer only, please.

She's a woman who is strong-willed		She's a desirable woman	❏
She's a woman who is needed by others	❏	She's a powerful woman	❏
She's a woman who is taken care of	❏	She's a passionate woman	❏
She's an adventurous woman	❏	She's a sensitive woman	❏

7. The following statements describe types or genres of books that you may be
interested in reading. Pick *up to 2 types* of books that you are most interested in.

I like to read about truly romantic relationships ❏
I like to read stories that are sexy romances ❏
I like to read romantic comedies ❏
I like to read a romantic mystery/suspense ❏
I like to read about romantic adventures ❏
I like to read romance stories that involve family ❏
I like to read about a romance in times or places that I have never seen ❏
Other: _____ ❏

*The following questions help us to group your answers with those readers who are
similar to you. Your answers will remain confidential.*

8. Please record your year of birth below.

19 _____

9. What is your marital status?

single ❏   married ❏   common-law ❏   widowed ❏
divorced/separated ❏

10. Do you have children 18 years of age or younger currently living at home?

yes ❏   no ❏

11. Which of the following best describes your employment status?

employed full-time or part-time ❏   homemaker ❏   student ❏
retired ❏   unemployed ❏

12. Do you have access to the Internet from either home or work?

yes ❏   no ❏

13. Have you ever visited eHarlequin.com?

yes ❏   no ❏

14. What state do you live in?

_____

15. Are you a member of Harlequin/Silhouette Reader Service?

yes ❏   Account # _____   no ❏   MRQ403SIM-1B

 **Silhouette®**

COMING NEXT MONTH

SIMCNM1003